Broken Wings

BILLIE ALLEN

Broken Wings

BY THE AUTHOR OF SUPERSTAR

TATE PUBLISHING
AND ENTERPRISES, LLC

Published by Tate Publishing & Enterprises, LLC
127 E. Trade Center Terrace | Mustang, Oklahoma 73064 USA
1.888.361.9473 | www.tatepublishing.com

Tate Publishing is committed to excellence in the publishing industry. The company reflects the philosophy established by the founders, based on Psalm 68:11,
"The Lord gave the word and great was the company of those who published it."

Book design copyright © 2014 by Tate Publishing, LLC. All rights reserved.
Cover design by Rtor Maghuyop
Interior design by Caypeeline Casas
Author photo courtesy of Anthony Bednar Photography

Published in the United States of America

ISBN: 978-1-63268-122-5
Fiction / Christian / General
14.04.15

Dedication

To Everyone who believed in me. A special thank you to Jonathan for the title, and Dr. Nathan Duer for his knowledge and humor. Any medical mistakes are mine.

Contents

ELEGY

I will not die but live,
and will proclaim what the Lord has done.
The Lord has chastened me severely,
but he has not given me over to death.

Psalm 118: 17–18

Felipe stared at the pills in his hand. They were so pretty, so lethal. One promised peaceful dreams; a whole handful the dreamless sleep of death.

The question was could he go through with it? Felipe was methodical and organized; he had planned the whole thing. He would swallow the pills and sangria and wake up in heaven with Adam, his beloved father. Marcos and Mallie would grieve, but they had each other and the baby. There was no one to mourn him because he had no one. He had broken up with Rosemary weeks ago. She would cry, yes, but she would get over him.

People wouldn't understand his reasons. He didn't care if Adam said his story was just beginning. He was talented, reasonably intelligent, and fairly good looking. He didn't lack for women, even though, except for Rosemary, they mostly bored him. Thanks to the band, he was even wealthy.

But he wasn't happy. He wasn't even content. How could they say he had everything when no one knew what everything was? They didn't know. Only Adam, with his love and wisdom, could help him—save him— as he had his brother, Marcos. Why wasn't his father here? Why had he left him?

Well, so be it, Felipe mused angrily. He would go to Adam.

But a minute later he flung the pills across the room and sent the glass shattering as his fist slammed against the table. Just like before, something was stopping him. *I can't do it,* he realized, disgusted. *I can't even swallow a few pills.*

Or was it someone didn't want him to?

⌁

"You can't keep going against me, Adam." The deep voice added reproachfully, "My other messengers respect me. They don't argue." He leaned forward. "They listen to what I tell them. No, it's only you and that bullheaded wife of yours that defy me!"

"'Tis sulking you are, Gabriel." Adam shook his blond head ruefully. "Not a very attractive quality in an angel."

"It's *archangel*, and you can stop with the brogue. This is Carlotta's doings, isn't it? You're protecting her."

"Of course I am." The teasing tone gone from his voice, Adam added flatly, "And I'm not letting her go back to earth by herself. Felipe is my child too."

"You two can't interfere this time."

"We already have. And you'll not be stopping us."

"You know the consequences, Adam," the archangel warned.

"I do." His chin set stubbornly. "And I don't care. I'm the only one Felipe will listen to."

"Arrogance is not an attractive quality in an angel either." He suddenly waved his arm, and Adam's customary overcoat abruptly vanished, to be replaced by a simple corduroy jacket. "Very well then. You have one day to change your mind. Beyond that I cannot help you. You and Carlotta will be banished."

"So be it." Adam bowed his head gravely.

"And may God have mercy upon your souls."

Befuddlement

"Your grandfather is an angel."

Mark O'Hara gazed down at his six-month-old daughter as he pondered his words. Carlie was a little young to be hearing such a startling confession. He certainly hadn't planned on telling her about Adam just yet, but it seemed, suddenly, that he should. A nudge, you might say. Nudges had become quite familiar to Mark ever since hurricane Adam had blasted into his life again. Though to be fair he had never needed his father more.

"He doesn't have wings or a halo," the superstar singer went on, holding out a rattle for Carlie to grab. "At least, I don't think he does. I suppose he could, but I've never seen them. Maybe some angels don't have wings."

"Da," said Carlie, waving the rattle.

"You don't think so, Carlita?" The last Mark had seen of his father, Adam, had been clad only in his grungy black overcoat and the blue jeans he had worn on his last day of work. It had turned out to be the last day of his life as well.

"I suppose you're going to think this is ridiculous, love, but he's been more of a father to me dead than alive," Mark went on. "I'm not saying he wasn't a good father, but I was eight years old when he...he died. He didn't have much of a chance to spend time with me or Felipe—Uncle Felipe," he corrected as Carlie's alert green eyes focused on him.

"He was always working. And that blasted factory killed him," he said grimly.

But death hadn't ended Adam's exuberant love for his son. He had found a way to be with Mark at the darkest hour of his life, making his presence known with the full force of his bold personality. He had coaxed, ordered, and charmed his way into his sons' hearts again, and never once had he revealed the truth to them—that he was not what he claimed and never would be.

"An angel without wings...I suppose it happens," Mark said musingly, shifting Carlie in his arms.

From out of nowhere, a deep Irish voice said reproachfully, "And what is this nonsense you're telling my wee granddaughter? Not have wings? Just because you're not seeing them, laddie, doesn't mean that I don't have them," Adam said as Mark gazed at him speechlessly, his mouth falling open.

But you don't, he realized. Not anymore. Gabriel had seen to that.

"Though there are some I could mention that certainly don't deserve them," he added darkly, straightening the unfamiliar and uncomfortable jacket as he sat down beside Mark.

"Papa?" Mark squeaked finally.

"Were you expecting someone else? I did tell you I would be back from time to time." Adam reached out and put a hand under Mark's chin. "You're looking like a deer caught in headlights, laddie."

Skin and bones and hair. He felt so normal, the singer realized, grabbing his father's hand tightly. His catechism at Perpetual Aggravation hadn't covered the anatomy of angels.

"Mark, I'm not going anywhere," said Adam, putting his other hand over his son's.

"You...you're not wearing the overcoat," his confused son blurted, staring at the corduroy coat.

Not yet ready to tell him what was going on, Adam said casually, "A change, you might say. 'Tis Carlie's doings. She will be trying to spiff me up."

"I don't understand. You...you said you would come when you were...were needed."

"And I have," Adam said simply.

"But I don't...I mean, I'm fine," Mark said, bewildered. But as the fog lifted, and he realized belatedly that others might need him, he gazed from Adam to Carlie, his hazel eyes suddenly wide with panic. No, not his baby...

"She's fine," his father said swiftly. "Would I be frightening you like that? She's—"

"Mallory?" demanded Mark, not caring if he interrupted or not. It didn't seem logical that his wife needed an angel's help. Not when she was well and happy and making tea for her parents in the kitchen. They had come all the way from Green Mountain, Vermont, to meet their first grandchild, and Mark wondered briefly just how he was going to explain Adam's presence.

Adam, who hadn't been in the living room ten minutes ago.

"You're jumping to conclusions—wrong ones." He held out his arms and Mark handed Carlie to him.

"If I am, it's because you're not telling me anything," the singer retorted.

"And you're not noticing anything. That's part of the problem." Adam gazed at his son in grave reproach. "You see him everyday and you look past him, Mark. You see him but you don't."

"Felipe?" He drew in his breath sharply. His little brother was in trouble, and Adam thought he wasn't frightening him? And how could he say that he looked right past him? *I don't do that*, Mark protested silently, his hands absently fingering the rattle. I may not have as much time for him since Carlie was born, but I don't ignore him. I couldn't.

"No, laddie?" Adam seemed to be following his thoughts again.

"I'm married now. I have a child. You can't expect me to spend as much time with him as I used to, Papa."

"I expect you to talk with him. I expect you to realize that something is very wrong." Adam's bright-blue eyes held him in place, daring him to offer other excuses. "Just as he did you."

"I realize that! I'm not deliberately—dios! What's wrong with him? I know he's been depressed lately but..." Mark's agitated words trailed off as he stared at

Adam's troubled features, a face devoid of its customary humor. "Papa…"

The words, when they finally came, chilled him. "He's been thinking of suicide."

Consternation

Why, you do not even know what will happen tomorrow.

What is your life? You are a mist that appears for a little while and then vanishes.

James 4: 14

Suicide.

The word kept echoing through his numb mind, torturing Mark with its very finality and ugliness. It was a word he had no familiarity with whatsoever.

No, not Felipe. Never his little brother.

"But that—that's a sin," he choked out finally. Adam had to be wrong, even if he was an angel.

"Paid attention to your catechism, did you?" Adam eyed him with a touch of pity. "Mark, I don't think Felipe cares about the 'rules.'" *No more than I do,* he added silently.

"But he…he wanted to be a priest. Don't you remember?"

"Aye. And I wanted to be an actor." The pity was replaced by exasperation. "Are you thinking priests can't be troubled and unhappy, laddie? Think again."

"No, of course not! I mean I don't know how to deal with this." He raked his fingers through his hair. "It's not possible...not Felipe! Papa, he's kept *me* sane over the years." Mark gazed at his father with bleak, angry eyes—eyes that demanded an explanation.

"Why? What is so devastating that he would ever—"

"Felipe doesn't have what you do."

"A wife and child? Papa, he's never wanted either! He runs from commitments. I think that's the reason he broke up with Rosemary. She wanted something more from him."

"He thinks he's not worthy of her." A slight sigh followed his admission. It was all he knew of the situation; Gabriel had allowed him no more information. Carlotta and he were entirely on their own.

"That's ridiculous. She's crazy about him."

"Since the lad has broken up with her, it's a moot point, son."

"Can't you...can't you fix him? Use your crystal ball, or whatever it is you do, and make him better," Mark pleaded.

Oh, if he only could. He didn't even know where Felipe was. "I wish I could. I wish it was that simple, but I know what I see, what I hear." Adam's somber blue eyes passed over his older son to focus on scenes too painful for a parent to see.

"I will not have my son turn into Sean," Adam said witheringly, thinking of his older brother. "Felipe is crying out for help, Mark, and you have to do something." His voice faltering, he added at last, "Because *I* can't."

Not really hearing Adam's last words, Mark shot back. "What would you like me to do, Papa? Get him therapy? Antidepressants? Or would you prefer I find him a woman?"

His father heaved an exasperated sigh." Marcos Adam Luis, are you not paying attention? You certainly aren't listening. That is not…" Adam stopped in mid sentence as the dining room door squeaked open and his daughter-in-law burst into the living room.

"Adam!" Mallory cried happily.

"Aye, love, and it's grand to see you again." Adam wrapped his free arm around her and kissed her affectionately.

Mallory gazed from him to her grim-faced husband and wondered what was wrong. Mark pouting? Was it possible? "Have I interrupted something?"

"Oh, just Papa scolding me. He thinks I'm still eight." Mark heard the door squeak again and shook his head slightly at his father. The two people in the doorway wore the same incredulous expression, and Adam was not slow to realize his unexpected appearance warranted an explanation. Now if he could only find one they would believe.

"Sure, and it's Mr. and Mrs. Kaplan, isn't it? You must be wondering where I got to that night in Vermont."

"You mean when you vanished without a word?" Lucas Kaplan said drily, remembering how he had searched for hours for the elusive Adam.

"I told you, Pop, that he talked to me," Mallory said hastily. Her arm was still around Adam, and she felt the slight tremor his body gave—strange how nervous he seemed. "He had a good reason."

"That I did." A shadow passed over his face as he sought the right words. "It was because of my wife." Two words he hadn't said aloud in a very long time, and yet they still felt so very right and natural, still held the pride he felt when he thought of Carlotta. "I had to go to her," he said simply.

"But I thought…" Mary Kaplan began, looking at Mark in total confusion. Surely he had told her he didn't have a mother. Even the wonderful interview Mallie had done with her superstar husband had mentioned it.

Funny, but she couldn't recall him mentioning Adam either.

And how had he appeared at Ambercrest so suddenly?

He didn't seem to even have a suitcase.

Her thoroughly bewildered son-in-law didn't know what to say. He knew all too well what he had told her—Carlotta had died of cancer when he was a teenager. He hadn't expected Adam to mention her at all; much less did Mark think Adam would own up to her very existence.

It appeared that was exactly what his father was doing.

"Papa," he said in a choked voice.

"Would you like to meet her?" Adam asked, his innocent question prompting a smothered gasp from his shocked son.

Meet her? Carlotta was *here*?

"Do you mean your wife, not Mark's mother?" Mary asked, thinking she had stumbled onto the solution. If he had simply remarried…

Adam lifted bushy blond brows and gave her a puzzled look. "I don't understand. I have but one wife, and my sons one mother."

"Papa," Mark tried again, his voice rising in panic.

"Laddie, there's no need to be fretting about your mama. Go upstairs and she'll tell you so." Adam gave him an innocent smile. "Perhaps you can explain the box on the wall."

"Box on the wall?" Mallory echoed as Mark got up hurriedly.

"Aye. The one that talks. It gave us quite a start." Of course his parents had never seen an intercom. Loquesta was lucky it had electricity.

In the entry, Mark had just started up the stairs when a slight noise startled him. He knew even before turning around that it was Carlotta. The scent of lavender wrapped around him like a comforting hug. A loving smile on her lips, she reached out both arms to her speechless son.

"You're here," he whispered at last. "You're really here…

"You were not expecting me?" she said in her soft voice as Mark abruptly hurled himself into her arms. "When my children need me, nothing else matters."

"How can this be happening?" her awestruck son whispered, clinging to her. "How can you be here?"

Ha! According to Gabriel and his rules, she shouldn't be. She should let some other messenger be sent to Felipe, her baby. Or worse yet, no one at all. The archangel just did not understand, Carlotta decided, stepping back to touch her son's dark curls.

"Marcos, I am not going anywhere," she said gently.

It was the same thing Adam had said, Mark remembered, perplexed.

"You're staying? You aren't going to…to disappear?" he said in a low voice.

"No," Carlotta said briefly, her eyes shadowed as she turned slightly away.

Something was wrong here. She was evading the subject.

"Mama? What aren't you telling me?"

She had forgotten just how intuitive Marcos was. But she wanted Adam present when she tried to answer her son's questions.

"Mama?" Mark repeated.

"Such a grand house you have, and so many rooms! Are they all yours?"

"You wouldn't tell me your name on the beach that night, and now this." Mark gave her an exasperated smile. "I know you. You're twirling your hair; you only do that when something is bothering you. But I suppose you'll tell me eventually." Still holding her hand in his, he added, "Yes, the whole house is mine. And the box on the wall is an intercom."

"Intercom," she repeated after he explained. Such a strange word.

"It's easier than yelling."

"My son, more successful than I ever dreamed possible." Carlotta shook her head in admiration. "Your papa has told me you are on the television. I should like to see this." As Mark turned red, his mother touched his cheek and firmly told him, "It is good that you are humble, Marcos, but you should also be very proud of what you have accomplished. From Loquesta to *this*?"

Before her thoroughly embarrassed son could respond, Adam came out of the living room, his normal smile vanishing as his blue eyes focused on them.

"We need to talk, laddie."

"Yes, we do." He shot a hurried glance at his watch. "Unfortunately, we can't do it now because I have to get to a sound check. I have a concert tonight." *And I can't leave you two here with Lucas and Mary,* he worried, *with only Mallory to field ticklish questions. Anything could happen and probably would.* "Maybe you could come along."

"We could," Adam said, adding playfully, "Or we could stay here and entertain your in-laws." He grinned. "They want to know what I've retired from, laddie."

"They what? Papa, what did you tell them?"

"Saving lost souls?" his father said innocently, taking his wife's hand.

"I've entered the twilight zone," the superstar groaned, staring at Adam in dismay. His father thought this was funny?

"Papa…"

"I'm an emissary from a higher power?" he said, and Carlotta burst into giggles. Evidently Adam thought it was hysterical.

"Papa! Will you please be serious?" Mark pleaded.

"You can't expect us not to have any fun, laddie."

"They're Mallory's parents! You show up out of the blue, without any luggage—"

"We travel light?" said a still giggling Carlotta.

"With a wife who's supposedly been *dead* for thirteen years—"

"Has it been that long?"

"Yes! And you ask them if they want to meet her? My mother? Papa, she looks like my little sister!"

"They're going to hear you, son."

"They're going to *see* Mama," Mark said flatly, "and wonder how she has a thirty-two-year-old son."

"The usual way," Carlotta said impishly, and Mark groaned and clapped a hand over his face.

"Fine talk coming from my mother." A ghost of a smile lit his face. "I give up. I don't know what to tell them so apparently we'll have to wing it, no pun intended." As Carlotta looked at him puzzledly, Mark added, "Improvise, Mama." He tucked her hand through his arm. "Let's go meet your granddaughter."

The twilight zone was an apt description for the meeting that followed.

Mark saw Mary's eyes widen in amazement as he introduced Carlotta to them. He watched as Lucas gazed at his petite black-haired mother in open admiration. And as Carlotta reached to take the wailing Carlie, his sense of shock and awe rose as his infant daughter immediately stopped crying and stared at her grandmother with a friendly expression.

How is it possible? How can Carlie—why, she knows *her*, Mark realized in bewilderment as Carlotta murmured something in Spanish and the baby cooed back at her. It was a sentiment Mary noticed as well.

"Why, she seems—"

"Carlotta has a grand way with babies," Adam cut in swiftly.

"I am afraid I spoiled both my sons," she said with her sweet smile.

"Especially Felipe," Mark muttered.

"Both of you. I always wanted a daughter." She glanced at Mary, her intuitive eyes sliding over her. "And you have six. I imagine having a boy will be a novel experience, yes?" Dead silence followed her soft question, then chaos erupted.

"Mama?" Mark said incredulously.

"Ma?" Mallory echoed in disbelief.

"Mary?" Lucas said, his mouth falling open in shock. "You're pregnant?"

"I just found out yesterday," his wife said, eying Carlotta as though she was a witch. "How could you have known?"

Seemingly unconcerned by the turmoil her innocent words had caused, Carlotta said, "You have a glow about you."

"But you said that…"

Far too much. Mark looked at Adam helplessly, imploring him to do something—anything—before the angelic Carlotta said something else.

"I imagine twins were an adventure?" Adam asked, playing along.

Lucas was still staring at his wife in stupefaction. It was Mallory, trying to distract them, who said hurriedly, "You have no idea, Adam. We're like oil and water. Rosemary was the free spirit and I was always trying to keep her out of trouble. Lost cause." She shrugged.

It appeared Mark's prayers weren't to be answered.

"You even took the driving test for her," Carlotta said innocently, and Lucas choked on his tea. Voices again erupted.

"Carlie…"

"How in the world—Mallory Elizabeth—"

"I told her! And I had to do it, Pop. Rosemary can't parallel park," Mallory said hurriedly as her father's eyes shot to her for an explanation.

"That is not—why am I even bothering?" Lucas looked so bewildered that a sympathetic Adam swiftly poured him a glass of sangria. "I'm thinking you need this," he said, and the other man gave a nod.

"More like the whole bottle." He fixed his eyes again upon his eldest daughter. "By the way, where is your sister, or should I just ask Carlotta?"

"I don't know," Mallory said helplessly. Rosemary was supposed to be here to see their parents, but she hadn't heard from her twin in hours. "I thought she was going to be here, but by all means ask Miss Wings." The words were out of her mouth before she realized what she had said. Her own private nickname for her angel mother-in-law, created when Carlotta had followed her everywhere and scolded her in the process for not being with Mark. *Ha! Let's see you get out of this one, Mallie.*

Her parents were already regarding Carlotta as
some sort of witch or psychic, thanks to her shock-
ing comments.

"Miss   Wings?"   Mary   echoed,   looking   at
Mallory dubiously.

"Uh, yes. She…she travels a lot. An awful lot,"
answered her uncomfortable daughter, looking at Mark
for help. He could try to say something, not sit there
like a frozen statue.

"They…they fly to different places," he muttered
finally. "All over the country."

"The world, laddie," Adam corrected. "You could say
we're on a honeymoon."

Lucas was studying the genial Irishman. There was
something very odd about Mark's father. Aside from
skipping out that night in Vermont to go to a wife that
was supposedly dead, he didn't look old enough to be
retired from anything. And how had they appeared at
Ambercrest so quickly?

As for Carlotta, had she given birth when she
was ten? There was neither a grey hair nor wrinkle to
be found.

Catching her father's eyes upon the serene Carlotta,
Mallory knew exactly what he must be thinking—she
looks younger than my daughter.

"Do something!" she hissed in Mark's ear.

"Like what?" But aware that a bad situation was
growing worse by the second, he hurriedly got up and
held his hand out to his mother.

"You haven't seen the kitchen yet, Mama. Let's go see it," Mark said brightly as she handed Carlie over to Mallory.

"May Adam come too?"

"Of course. In fact, I insist on it."

They were barely in the kitchen when he demanded, "What's going on? Why are you two deliberately playing with them?" He didn't know whether to be angry or laugh along when Carlotta suddenly burst into giggles again.

"Mama, it's not funny. You told Mary that she's pregnant!"

"But she is," his mother answered.

"Didn't you think she might like to tell Lucas first?" As Adam started to laugh, his son heaved a sigh of exasperation. "Never mind. You will have your fun whatever I say."

"Aye. And you should be thinking about our problem, laddie."

"I have…sort of."

"Oh?" Adam eyed him gravely, the laughter gone from his eyes. "Are you sure? I don't think Felipe will appreciate being put on the spot, Mark. He doesn't crave the limelight as you do."

"You got a better idea?"

"No," Adam admitted. "That I don't. It's worth a try."

The superstar suddenly grinned playfully. "I'm glad you feel that way, Papa, because I'm putting you on the spot as well."

"What's that you're saying, laddie?" Adam looked from Carlotta to his son, his face mirroring confusion and dismay. "You can't be meaning..."

"Can't I? Go practice the Molly Macrae, Papa"— Mark put an arm around him—"because you and Felipe are both singing with me tonight!"

Surprise

"Sing?" Adam echoed, paling. "Before an audience?"

It seemed his father had a bad case of stage fright.

"You won't even know they're there. And you love to sing, Papa."

"Aye...in the kitchen, laddie. Not in front of hundreds of people," Adam protested.

Actually it was thousands, but he wasn't about to tell him that.

"And I'm not knowing any of your music."

"Well, I know yours. Pick whatever you like," Mark said firmly.

Carlotta turned from studying the vast array of pots and pans to say quietly, "But Felipe does not know it."

"He's a fast learner, Mama. And he knows the Molly Macrae; he's sung it with us. The problem is he's not going to want to." Felipe didn't seem to want to do anything anymore.

"You're right," he told his father somberly, feeling ashamed. "I should have seen it." *Was it too late?*

Adam looked at Carlotta; his blue eyes holding hers in a silent message.

"You forget, amado," she said sadly, shaking her head. "Felipe does not even realize that I exist. Why should he listen to me?"

"Carlie…"

"There is no need to look at me like that, Adam. You know very well that I will talk to him." A little catch in her voice, she added, "I did choose to do this."

"Am I missing something?" Mark asked curiously.

For the first time, he was becoming conscious of the uneasy expressions they both wore, and he remembered how emphatically his father had insisted that *he* do something.

Because Adam couldn't.

"You want to tell me what's going on?" He reached out and caught Carlotta's hand. "Stop playing with your hair and talk to me. What are you doing that you shouldn't?"

"I thought you said you had to check the music," she said.

"Sound check," the singer corrected. "And I'll make the time. Are you two playing hooky from heaven?"

"Hooky?" Carlotta echoed, confused.

"Not exactly, laddie," Adam said slowly. "The truth is, Mark, we're not really supposed to be here."

"You weren't sent here?"

"Not this time. And we're breaking all the rules by staying here."

"Oh, blast Gabriel and his rules!" Carlotta snapped.

"Carlie," said Adam helplessly as his wife burst into tears.

"I am still his mother! But does Gabriel understand *that*? No, he just yells about ancient laws and regulations!" Hiccoughing, she added, "We are doing this together, Marcos. Your father knew I had to do something—find some way to stop Felipe…" Her voice faltered and softened. "We have stopped him twice. The next time…"

"There isn't going to be a next time." The superstar added gently, "I made you a promise a long time ago, and I'm making it to you again." He smiled slightly. "I may have to beat him up a little in the process, but I will look after him."

"Are you thinking you have a choice, laddie?" Adam grinned.

"I suppose not. Not with the two of you ganging up on me."

"Marcos," Carlotta said abruptly, looking puzzled. "The refrigerator is leaking. And why is it making such a strange noise?"

"It makes ice cubes, Mama." He turned her around to face him. "Felipe's never seen you?" As she shook her head, he added, "Why not? Or aren't you allowed to tell me?"

"There is no great mystery. Felipe does not believe," she said simply. Still curious about the unusual refrigerator, she touched a button on the panel gingerly.

"It does not need ice trays, Marcos?"

"No, it's…" Mark stopped in mid answer as his up-to-now-normal refrigerator suddenly began shooting ice cubes at his unsuspecting mother.

"Aye de mi!" she cried, darting behind Adam.

And as suddenly as it began, the barrage of ice cubes stopped.

"Mama?" Mark went to her worriedly. "Are you all right?"

"I do not like the refrigerator." She peeped around Adam, gazing at the ice cubes on the floor.

"It's never done that before," said her mystified son.

Odd, Mark was still thinking a short time later at the sound check. *Adam had been strangely silent during the fiasco. Odder still that the ice cubes had vanished so quickly. It was almost as though he had expected something like that to happen. What rules were they breaking?* Mark wondered, going through a few bars of "Scandal." For that matter, who the heck was Gabriel? The only Gabriel he knew was the young priest from Loquesta.

"Felipe isn't here," Evan, his musical director, said behind him. "He forgot what time it is?"

Mark set his guitar back on the stand and scowled. "Evan, he's been forgetting what day it is."

He had left Adam and Carlotta in his dressing room; his mother amazed at the array of food, his father intrigued by the computerized equipment, and Mark wondered how Felipe would react to seeing their parents, especially Carlotta, his younger than young mother. How would any of them react?

"He's here," Evan's relieved voice broke into his thoughts. "Doesn't look very happy."

He didn't look very healthy either, his worried brother noted—bloodshot eyes, a pallor to his skin, and a general air of I-don't-care-and-you-can't-make-me about him; hair that looked as though it hadn't been washed or even combed in days; clothes that weren't buttoned; and not surprising, a very distinct odor of alcohol.

He stopped in front of his brother, hands on hips.

"Well, if it isn't Mr. Legend," he drawled, and Mark flinched.

"Nice of you to finally show up, Uncle Sean."

"Say what? What are you babbling about, Marcos?"

"Go take a look in the mirror. And while you're at it, take a shower," Mark ordered, wrinkling his nose in disgust.

"You forget we have a show later?" Evan asked curtly.

"So I lost track of time. I'm here." He leaned against his keyboard, trying to steady himself. "And what would it matter if I wasn't? It's your show, Marcos."

It seemed Adam was right again.

"Felipe, I've never been able to do this without you...I couldn't." He turned back to Evan. "Let's run through this since Felipe's decided to grace us with his presence."

"Oh, stuff it, Marcos," Felipe snapped wearily, not really hearing his brother's heartfelt words. He didn't care what they said to him. He only knew he didn't want to be here.

But a commotion behind him startled him out of his lethargy, and he staggered slightly as he faced an impossible sight.

Adam...*here*? How?

The security guards surrounded him.

"'Tis a fine kettle of fish, keeping me from my sons." He reached out to Mark, and the amused singer drew him forward.

"It's okay, guys. Find him a pass, please. This is our father."

"Father?" Evan said in disbelief, looking from Adam to his two sons. "Mark, this is the man who was in the wings last year."

So Evan had noticed and remembered.

"I know," Mark said, adding swiftly, "He's singing with me, Ev. Felipe too."

"You sure about that, amigo? Felipe doesn't look like he can even talk, let alone sing."

Mark couldn't see his brother's white incredulous face. He only saw Adam shake his head reproachfully as he gazed at his disheveled younger son and sighed. Uncle Sean part two.

"Papa?" Felipe choked out finally. "You're here?"

"Will I be going through this again?"

"You…you're not wearing the overcoat," Felipe said, trying to focus on him.

His confused mind remembered Adam never took it off. According to Mallie, he couldn't.

"Aye. And you appear to be wearing quite a bit of Jack Daniels," Adam said in disapproval, flinching from the strong smell.

"He can sing?" Evan said to Mark, eying Adam doubtfully.

"Oh, yes," his friend said reverently.

Papa was singing? Felipe wondered in confusion, not sure of his jumbled thoughts or anything else, for that matter. He only knew that his father was scolding him.

"It's…it's beer," Felipe said, his bottom lip quivering. "I fell. I was trying to hurry."

If I could only do something, a frustrated Adam despaired. "I'm disappointed in you, laddie." He turned to Mark. "You can't be letting him do a show in his condition. He needs to get cleaned up."

"There's not that much time, Papa."

"You don't need me," said his woebegone brother, looking ready to cry.

"Oh, yes, I do," Mark said. "Weren't you listening? We're singing together."

"You mean you and Papa," Felipe managed.

"Now, would I be leaving you out when you've got a voice as well?" demanded Mark, his brogue mimicking Adam's.

"But I can't—me?" Felipe was panic-stricken, bewildered, and nauseated at the same time. Didn't they realize he could barely stand up? Was this some sort of sick joke?

"Papa, I cannot sing. I'm drunk."

"Aye. So you are." Adam's blue eyes shone with pain. "And I will not let you become another Sean. My brother, God rest his soul, did not have your talent, laddie. You have music in your blood, not whiskey." Under his breath, he muttered, "He couldn't even identify my body."

"Papa…"

"You haven't realized it yet." He put both hands on his son's shaking shoulders. "Felipe, you're an O'Hara too."

Was he? Felipe heard Adam's words, the pride in his voice, but his thoughts were in a much earlier time—Loquesta—where olive-skinned and dark-haired children roamed the streets, and a small blue-eyed blond boy was an outcast. He had never belonged, never fit in like Marcos had.

"Stega! Pretty little white boy!"

It was a word Felipe loathed—an outsider.

Day after day, he had come home bruised and bloody, his spirits broken as he tried to keep the vile knowledge from Carlotta, who was already feeling the effects of cancer. At first he had even tried to keep it from his brother, until one day...

"Who did this to you?" Marcos demanded.

"Scum. It doesn't matter, Marcos."

"What kind of rot is that? Of course it matters!" Nearly blind with rage, his brother hissed, "They won't be bothering you anymore—not if I have anything to say about it!"

"But you can't just—"

"Watch me."

Even at such a young age, Marcos had already begun to fight; the knife that was a part of his arm never far from his hand. It puzzled Felipe.

"But you don't like to fight. You hate violence."

"I hate being afraid more."

Ah. That was a concept that made sense to the young and impressionable Felipe. Without Adam to guide him, he had soon focused a hero's worship on Marcos. His brother was more and more assuming a role as head of the family. It was a responsibility he did not take lightly.

"Mama has enough on her plate without worrying that you'll get cut one night. Stay away from these... these cabrons," he spat the word viciously. "I can't always be there to protect you."

"Then I better learn to do it myself."

And so it had begun. He was thin and small, but Felipe possessed a wiriness and speed that soon overcame his opponents. He was also graceful, not unlike his brother.

"You planning on taking down everyone who called you a half-breed, hermanito?" Marcos asked in alarm.

"Is there some reason why I shouldn't? You would," he pointed out, and Marcos agreed.

It was an existence that culminated the night Tonio and his cronies had ambushed Marcos—the night the world had turned upside down and inside out for Felipe. Adam was gone, Carlotta lived in a wasted body, and now his brother was bleeding to death in an alley. What the hell had happened? Was God punishing him for no longer wanting to be a priest? Was he that vindictive?

"Let him live and I'll do whatever you want!" he had cried, dropping onto his knees in the filthy street. He spared not even a backward glance at the bloody body of his tormentor as he flung out his hand. As far as he was concerned, justice had been done.

He had never told Marcos about the words he had heard in his ear—words that he later realized were Adam's.

"Can you really be thinking God wants him to die, laddie?" A powerful warmth seemed to infuse him. "Go now, Felipe. You're in danger here."

"But I can't just—"

"Now, laddie."

Arguing with heavenly beings was not something they had recommended in catechism. Felipe went back to Marcos, stunned to see that his brother had fashioned a bandage from his shirt and was trying to stand up.

"You're okay. You're not dead."

"Neither are you. You seem to be in one piece."

Felipe had tried to smile. "One down and one to go. Let's see him try anything now."

So long ago, and yet he could still feel the blessed relief in his body and taste the tears on his face. The voice had been right—his brother was alive.

And so he had made a promise.

"But I don't know what to do," Felipe, the boy and the man, whispered. Was this why God had stopped him? Was he meant to sing like his brother?

Like someone coming out of a trance, he blinked and seemed to shake himself as he stared at the mike Mark was holding out.

"Papa..." he began, feeling very helpless.

"Trust me, laddie."

Maybe this is a dream, Felipe decided, reluctantly taking the mike, *and it's not really happening at all.*

"Fine, I'll sing. And I don't really care if I screw up because this isn't real."

"Papa, you real?" Mark handed Adam a mike as well.

"As real as you, laddie."

"Then let's show them how it's done." He counted down the beats, and right on cue, the three of them broke into the Molly Macrae, their voices syncing perfectly. They went through two verses of the old Irish folk ballad as Evan and the rest of the band regarded them in open shock and disbelief.

"Holy shit," Evan breathed, his mouth hanging open. His doubts about Adam's singing ability had vanished completely.

"If Hank hears him, he'll sign him to a contract."

The amused superstar set the mike down and said, "I did tell you. That song is a part of our childhood, Ev. My mother used to get upset that he was teaching us bar songs." Mark looked past Adam and Felipe to see that Carlotta had ventured out of his dressing room and was quietly standing in the wings, her eyes fixed on Felipe. The time had come.

Excusing themselves from the band, Mark nudged Adam.

"I know, laddie." He heaved a sigh. In a solemn voice, he told his younger son,

"I'm not here alone, Felipe."

Still amazed that he had remembered the words, Felipe said absently, "There's no one here but us, Papa, except for that girl who's staring at me."

"So you do see her?"

Felipe stared at him. "Is there a reason why I shouldn't, Marcos? I'm drunk, not hallucinating."

"Maybe you should go talk to her."

"Have you gone around the bend? I don't know how she got in here, Marcos, but I do not hang out with groupies"—he gave a little shudder—"no matter how pretty they are."

"Groupies?" Mark made a face. "Felipe, she's not…"

"Better you should let me explain, Mark." He nudged his older son in Carlotta's direction, and as Felipe eyed him expectantly, Adam sighed again and finally muttered, "'Tis difficult to find the words." He reached over to lay his hand on his son's shoulder.

"Felipe, she's your mother."

Rejection

His mother?

"Is this some kind of joke?" Felipe demanded, his icy blue eyes fixed on Adam's. "I don't find this funny, Papa." A sob choked his voice. "How could you even say—"

"Because it's the truth," Adam snapped, incensed that he would doubt him. "Are you thinking I'm making up stories now?"

"I think I should know my own mother!" Felipe retorted, shaking off Adam's arm.

"And I certainly should know my wife!" his father roared, losing his temper.

"Uh oh," Mark said, hurriedly moving forward. Was he supposed to play referee?

"Papa, you've lost it," his brother shot back, his angry eyes focused on the girl.

Long black hair that floated around her slender shoulders, her face serene as she gazed back at him; a somewhat dated blue-and-white dress that seemed oddly familiar but suited her tiny figure. And as he watched in frozen fascination, she held out her hand to him.

"No!" Felipe cried, backing away in horror. That there was something vaguely familiar about her he ignored;

he would not believe this—this girl could be his mother. Having never seen a picture of Carlotta when she was younger, he refused to believe it. He tripped over the cables on the floor and would have fallen if Mark hadn't caught him.

"She is Mama," his brother said quietly.

"You've both gone crazy!" He saw Adam had his arm around her.

And he had trusted him!

"I've got to get out of here." He tried to turn away but Mark had too firm a grip.

"Oh no, you don't. You think Papa is hugging a stranger?" he snapped, his own temper beginning to unravel. "Is it proof you want—you who won't believe anything but black and white? No shades of grey for you, Felipe."

As Felipe gazed sullenly at the girl, she stepped toward him.

"I suppose you're an angel too?" he demanded.

"I am not here as a messenger," she frowned, moving closer. "And I have had enough. You will not speak to me in that fashion, Felipe. I *am* your mother and I came here hoping that you would listen to me—since you apparently will not to anyone else. What is this blasphemy about suicide?" she said, crossing her arms and daring him to contradict her.

Every vestige of color drained from his face. He opened his mouth to speak, to tell this familiar stranger that she didn't understand, but Carlotta was far from finished.

"You would throw your life away just like that? What God has given you? What I lost to the cancer you would give up willingly?" She shook her head in disgust. "Felipe Sean Miguel, I never spanked you but I am sorely tempted now."

How could she know his names? How could any of this be happening?

"You don't understand," Felipe managed to protest, backing away from his tiny tormentor. He gazed at Mark for help, certain that she would indeed try to spank him, but his brother was hiding behind Adam, half afraid he would be next.

"Bastante! So I do not understand? Do you think I did not know how unbearable things were for you in Loquesta? Did you give up then? When Marcos was stabbed and you had no money or food, did you run away? To just throw in the rag and curl up in the corner? No, that did not occur to either of you, did it?"

"Towel, Mama," Mark said hesitantly, still peering around Adam.

"Gracias, Marcos. Well, Felipe?"

"Who *are* you? Who told—"

"I do not need to be told; I know. I saw what you did. I heard everything." She suddenly reached out and grabbed his arm, gesturing to a small scar on his wrist. "Do you not remember how you got this? You were six years old and burned yourself with cocoa." Carlotta saw him blanch at her words. "I suppose you think someone told me that as well?"

The mother he remembered had yellowish eyes and skin and had shrunk to nearly a skeleton. He gazed at this beautiful young woman and shuddered at the injustice.

"I-I don't know what to think."

"You killed Tonio's friend to avenge your brother."

"Marcos could have…" his words trailed off as even in his alcohol-shrouded mind he realized how implausible that was. Carlotta had been dying when the assault happened; Marcos wouldn't have her told her anything like that. "I don't know how you know that," he said, eying her uncertainly. "Or the cocoa. And how can angels condone killing?" Felipe added reproachfully.

"They do not. I am speaking as your mother, if you would only listen."

"Hey, I'm listening. You came because of me, because you think I'm going to kill myself." As the sudden, conflicting emotions tumbled through his mind, Felipe shook his head and tried to compose himself. "Yeah, well, I couldn't even do that right," he said scornfully. But as the fog in his brain lifted somewhat, he blinked and turned to Adam, saying flatly, "Because of you. You stopped me, Papa."

"No, Felipe," Adam said shortly, still angry at his son's cavalier attitude. "Carlie stopped you."

And he was supposed to be grateful? "Third time's the charm," he said, and Carlotta looked like she was about to cry.

"Felipe!" Mark hissed just as Mallory suddenly appeared on the stage.

"My parents are looking after Carlie; trying to get in practice again." She smiled at her mother-in-law. "They think you're some sort of witch, Miss Wings." Her eyes traveled from Carlotta's troubled face to Felipe's ashen features, and she said puzzledly, "This doesn't seem like a happy family reunion. What's wrong?"

"My son does not want to know me," said Carlotta as Felipe continued to stare at her.

"My mother is dead!" The ragged grief still gripped him as he muttered, "We…buried her."

"And I wore a blue-and-white dress. Do you not recognize it, Felipe?" She gestured at her dress. "I held a rosary in my hands—_this_ one." Carlotta suddenly thrust her hand at her son.

Felipe took one look at the beads curled in her palm, the worn initials C.O. still visible, gave a choked cry and slumped to the floor.

"History repeats itself," Mark said, barely managing to catch him. "Remember, Papa?"

"Aye. I will be getting the brandy," Adam said ruefully, recalling a bottle in the dressing room.

Heedless of the dirty floor, Carlotta dropped down beside Felipe, her hand moving gently over his ashen face. "So it has come to this," she murmured quietly. "I did not wish to shock him but I had no choice; he would not listen." His eyes were fluttering and she gave an anguished sigh at how very bloodshot they were.

And there is nothing you can do as an angel. Perhaps not even as a mother.

She, too, was thinking of Sean. "Has he been drinking a lot, Marcos?"

"He…he doesn't keep me informed of his activities, Mama," Mark answered, hoping she would not pressure him. He did not want to tell her that his brother had taken to nearly living at Infinity, closing the club practically every night. Felipe was past caring what his family thought of him; his solace and his life were rapidly centering on the whiskey bottles that littered his very existence.

But she should already know that, he told himself as Felipe's eyes blinked open.

Adam held out the brandy bottle. "There's a wee bit left, but I was not finding a glass."

"I don't need one," Felipe muttered, carefully avoiding Carlotta's eyes. He sat up gingerly and all but snatched the bottle from Adam. Only when he had drained it did he finally gaze at his mother.

"So what's next, *Mother*? Do I sit here and listen to you preach religious nonsense to me? Are you going to absolve me of my sins?" Standing, he added almost thoughtfully, "What you don't seem to realize is that it's *my* life and I'll do what I want with it, whatever that may be. I haven't decided yet." He smirked his indifference. "But I'll be sure to let you know."

"Felipe!" cried his aghast brother.

"You think I care, Marcos? Here's a newsflash for you—I don't care about anything." He added disdainfully "I'll be at Infinity, or maybe that new club, Hell. Hey, that's funny. Angels and Hell don't exactly mesh, do they?"

"We have a concert," Mark hissed.

"Maybe I'll be there, maybe I won't. You and Papa can handle it. Adios."

In the silence that followed the sound of the stage door slamming, Carlotta choked back a helpless sob and covered her face with her hands. "I have messed up everything."

"You did nothing of the kind." Mark went to her quickly and hugged her. "Felipe is just being melodramatic as usual; he's not going to kill himself, Mama."

"I wouldn't take this lightly, Mark," Mallory said soberly. "He's in nine kinds of pain and he doesn't know why." She shook her head. "You can't just ignore it; he needs help."

"I'm not ignoring it. I'm going to talk some sense into him, hopefully." He held out his hand to his wife. "Care to come with me, love?" Mark smiled mirthlessly. "Someone has to protect me from the groupies and keep me from throttling him. Besides, you've never been to Infinity."

Neither had he, for that matter. Mark stared around him at the glass dance floor, the bar that stretched the full length of the room, and the mirrors that seemed to be everywhere—like an optical illusion, he mused, realizing the reason for the club's name. Why, it was making him slightly dizzy.

"Do you see him?" Mallory said, raising her voice above the music.

"In this crowd? Who can find anyone?" The club was packed with people, and quite a few of them were staring at Mark incredulously. Oh God, not now, he prayed. He had no desire to sign any autographs or pictures; he wanted to find Felipe and get back to the theater.

He smiled nervously and steered his wife in another direction.

"This place is neat!" she yelled in his ear.

"We'll come back."

"Now I know why Rosemary likes it. Hey, I think I see him!" Mallory tugged on his hand, leading her nervous husband to yet another section of the crowded club, a quieter one. Here the music was not so loud, and there were tables to be had. As luck would have it, they found the same one where Felipe was sprawled.

He didn't notice them at first. His eyes were closed, and he seemed to be listening to the music, swaying slightly. A bottle and glass were before him on the table, and Mark eyed it in disbelief. He was drinking sangria.

"No, it's not whiskey." Felipe opened his eyes. "Surprised, Marcos?"

"Should anything you do surprise me?"

"I suppose not. What the hell are you doing here? You hate clubs." His lip curled. "You do realize that there are people here who recognize you, don't you? You know, the kinds with cameras and pictures and underwear." He shook his head. "Better run while you still can."

"Underwear?" echoed Mallory.

"You don't want to know, amada," Mark said hastily.

Felipe turned to gaze at her. "So you're here, too, Mallie. Gee, why didn't you bring the whole family? Papa and the pretty little girl who thinks she's my mother? Or don't angels dance?"

Mallory sat down beside him. "I don't know why you're doubting her, Felipe, but Miss Wings is telling you the truth. I spent enough time with her last year to know that she couldn't lie even if she wanted to." She turned to glance at Mark puzzledly. "There is one thing that's different, honey. Why aren't they, uh, popping in and out like they were before?"

Dear Lord, she was right, the startled superstar realized. The only time Adam had "popped in" was when he had first arrived at Ambercrest, presumably with Carlotta in tow. They had ridden to the theater with him, and Adam had said he wanted to return to Ambercrest to change for the concert. But why was it necessary to go home? He could snap his fingers, or whatever he did, to change.

"Change…" Mark stared off into the distance, not really hearing Felipe at first.

"If she's really an angel, why can't she fix me? Where's her wings?"

Mark had asked the same thing. Adam had wings but you couldn't see them, whereas Carlotta didn't seem to have any.

Or they were clipped.

"Broken wings," the superstar said softly, coming to a startling conclusion.

"They can't fix you," he said, shoving his chair back. "They can't do anything, Felipe." He reached out and yanked his brother to his feet. "And it's all because of you. They broke the rules…for you." He let go of his startled brother and urged Mallory upward. "We've got to get back, Mallory. It may be too late already."

"Too late for what?"

Mark eyed him angrily. "I left them in the parking garage, and they can't drive!"

⟋⟍

Across town, still in the garage, Adam was realizing the same thing. Though he had assured his son that it wouldn't be a problem to drive Mallory's car back to Ambercrest, his lack of technical knowledge regarding the cars of today was frustrating, indeed.

"There are too many buttons!" *And just where was the ignition,* he wondered, suddenly recalling Mallory hadn't given him a key. How was he supposed to start the engine?

He had driven in Ireland as a teenager and during his stint in the military. Even in Loquesta he had had an old car. But this sleek BMW was complicated, he frowned, pushing another button. The engine roared to life and he confidently pressed another. The blast of cold air startled him.

"Air conditioning?" questioned Carlotta.

"So it would seem, love. Well, let's try this one." He pushed another button and a small silver disc slowly slid forward, puzzling them both. They stared at it intently.

"It seems to have Mark's picture on it." Adam picked it up gingerly and studied it.

"Adam, there is a whole case of them," Carlotta said, pointing. "What are they?"

Adam was still studying the disc he held. "'Scandal.' Mark has a song called that. Could this be music?"

"But it is much too tiny to be a record. And where does it play?"

Not having an answer and deciding the discs were harmless, he set it aside and searched the car's interior. If there were only one of those pocket telephones both his sons had carried.

"Pocket telephones?" Carlotta echoed in disbelief.

"Aye, love. 'Tis wonderful they are, and so convenient."

"But you do not know his number," she pointed out. "And Mallory probably has hers in her own pocket." She shook her head in frustration. "Adam, we are not getting anywhere. You were a pilot; you flew in the war. You even drove in Loquesta. Can you not figure this out?"

Before he could answer, there was a tap on the window. A very frustrated Adam, not finding the handle, opened the door to one of the young men from the sound check.

"You're Mr. O'Hara, aren't you? I'm Ryan Potter, Mark's drummer."

"Aye," Adam said gratefully, "and it's glad I am to see you. This is my wife, Carlotta."

This girl was Mark's mother? Deciding she must have had the superstar when she was twelve, Ryan merely smiled politely and motioned to the BMW. "Are you having a problem with the car?"

"We do not know how to drive," Carlotta told him.

"And there are too many buttons!"

"We wanted to return to Ambercrest while Marcos looks for Felipe."

"You're not having one of those pocket telephones, laddie?" Adam asked hopefully.

"Pocket...oh, you're talking about a cell phone." Ryan grinned. "Sure, I do. But I think it would be better if I just drove you back to the house and waited for you. I'll call Mark and let him know so he doesn't worry."

Relieved, Adam willingly got in the backseat and watched curiously as Ryan put the car in gear and drove it out of the underground garage. So that was how it was done. He stored the information away and reminded himself he would have to practice, especially since they wouldn't be leaving here anytime soon, if ever.

"Laddie, would you be telling us what that thing is?" He motioned to the silver discs.

"And why does it have our son's picture on it?" Carlotta added.

Maybe they didn't get out much, Ryan decided, trying to remember what Mark had told him about his parents. Ryan had always assumed they were dead. Had he said anything at all?

Like they've lived in a cave or deserted island.

"Uh...it's a CD player. Compact disc," he added hastily, seeing Carlotta's puzzlement. "It has music on it."

"See, Carlie?" Adam said from the backseat.

"But it is not a record. How does something so tiny play music?"

Records? That does it, Ryan vowed. *I have to talk to Mark about these two.* He slid the disc forward and pushed the play button.

"They, uh, don't make records anymore, Mrs. O'Hara. These have far better sound quality. This one is Mark's latest." Ryan shook his head in admiration as his friend's pure and hauntingly beautiful voice filled the interior of the car. "Every time I hear Mark I get chills. He's got the voice of an angel."

As Carlotta smiled proudly, Adam said, "I would not be arguing with you, laddie."

"And I can see where he gets his talent, sir. That song you guys did was awesome. I hope you do it again."

"I'm afraid that depends on Felipe," Adam said ruefully.

"What the hell do you mean 'broke the rules'? What rules?" Felipe demanded, following his brother and Mallory from the club.

"I don't know. They aren't talking about it," Mark said tersely, practically running to the Porsche. He had to find Adam and Carlotta before it was too late. He felt utterly helpless. Maybe he was wrong. Maybe there was a perfectly simple explanation for Adam insisting there was nothing he could do for Felipe, or shedding his overcoat when he had never taken it off before.

They had assured him that they weren't going anywhere.

Because they *couldn't*.

In another part of the city, someone was going somewhere. Jerry Mendoza had brazenly slipped away from the prison work detail. He had been fortunate in that they were picking up the litter along the beach; he had merely found his way into a convenient port-a-potty, stripped off the prison jumpsuit, and casually mingled into the crowd of swimmers and sun worshipers. Once away from the other inmates, he strolled along the beach, taking a can of pop from one blanket and managing to find terry pants and a tank top from another. In the pocket he struck gold—there was a nice wad of cash, more than enough to sustain him until he accomplished his objectives.

Last year he had merely drugged and humiliated Mark O'Hara. This time he was going to kill him.

Panic

Earthbound angels—was it possible? Was that the real reason Adam wasn't wearing his tattered old overcoat?

"You are coming with me to the theater," Mark said to his sullen brother, determined to talk to Adam as soon as possible. "I'm not asking you to do the concert—I'm telling you. You aren't getting a free ride."

"Yes, sir," Felipe said mockingly.

"Stuff it. Stop having a pity party. Don't you realize that Mallory's right? They aren't 'popping' in and out anymore, because they *can't*," the superstar said flatly. "They aren't angels anymore, Felipe."

Felipe eyed his brother witheringly, finding the comment ridiculous. "Right."

"See if I'm wrong. Talk to…" his words trailed off as Mallory abruptly handed her phone to him.

"It's Ryan," she said, "and he's got Adam and Miss Wings with him. They couldn't get my car out of the garage. Something about buttons, I think?"

"See?" Mark said smugly. To his drummer he said in relief, "Amigo, you have no idea how grateful I am. I completely forgot that he doesn't drive…anymore," he added hastily, feeling a need to explain. "Would you mind taking them to Ambercrest and then the theater? I'll meet you there."

"I already am. It's no problem. Oh, and Adam wants a pocket telephone, by the way," Ryan said laughing. "Might be a good idea, Mark. See you at the theater."

Why would an angel want a phone? Was he planning on calling heaven?

"It seems Papa wants a cell phone."

A confused Felipe blurted, "But he doesn't need one! He—he whispers—he…" As the truth finally penetrated his alcohol-shrouded brain, he slumped against the seat, eying Mark in mingled guilt, despair, and astonishment.

"Now do you believe me?"

"He can't do this!" There was a trace of the old Felipe as he forced himself to sit up and face his brother. "Not for me. I'm not worth it."

It was a sentiment he later echoed to his father.

"Papa, I will not let you do this." He faced Adam in the wings, absently noting that his father was alone.

"Oh, really, laddie?" Adam was relieved to see that his younger son was actually sober and was even dressed neatly. "I have no idea what you're talking about, but I'm thinking I don't need your permission to do anything."

Keeping his voice low, Felipe blurted, "You've left heaven."

"Since you're seeing me, Felipe, technically I have left it."

"Permanently!"

"Ah," said Adam as Mark joined them. "I will be telling both of you, then, that the choice was mine."

"What about Mama?" Mark asked abruptly. And just where was Carlotta?

"Carlie is my wife. She goes where I go. And I want to see my grandchildren," Adam said simply.

Grandchildren? Mark echoed. Mallory wasn't pregnant, was she?

"Papa," he began.

"Shouldn't you two get out there?" his father asked pointedly.

The exasperated superstar said a quick prayer and ran onstage. Felipe said casually, "Just where is…Mother?"

"Helping Mallory mop up the kitchen. The dishwasher overflowed," Adam answered, looking troubled.

Felipe gave him a strange look before he too hurried onstage.

Left alone for the moment, Adam said tersely, "Carlie is not scared by a little water, Gabriel. I suppose you think it is funny?"

The archangel immediately appeared, his robes swirling around him.

"Adam, you know I would never hurt one of my messengers—ex-messengers, it seems."

"She was soaked!"

Gabriel strolled over to the edge of the wings, his eyes on Mark and Felipe.

"Magnificent," he murmured before turning back to Adam. "Your sons are concerned about you. Felipe believes he's unworthy of your sacrifice."

"They're good lads," said Adam. "And Felipe is wrong. My children are worth everything to me."

"Are they? We'll see." The archangel disappeared before Adam could question his enigmatic words and ponder what else was going to happen.

As it turned out, he hadn't long to wait.

⸺

Nearing the end of the concert, Mark was ebullient. There was only "Scandal" and the Irish medley with Adam and Felipe. His brother was playing the keyboard effortlessly and looked more like himself than he had in weeks.

So why did he have this feeling that things were going too well?

The opening chorus of "Scandal" began and his voice emerged as a squeal.

He couldn't sing.

The bewildered superstar dropped the mike and clutched his throat with both hands.

"Mark? What's wrong?" his stunned musical director demanded.

What was wrong indeed. He had never taken his voice for granted, never had any problems—until now.

"Get Felipe," Mark managed to mutter. So he could talk, at least.

His brother had already left his keyboard. "Marcos, this isn't funny," he began, then stopped as he saw the terror in Mark's hazel eyes.

My worse nightmare, the superstar thought helplessly. *I'm onstage and I can't sing.*

"Take over."

Turning pale, Felipe blurted, "Me—sing 'Scandal'? Have you lost your mind?"

"I've lost my voice." He shoved the mike at Felipe. Before any of them could say a word, Mark turned and ran from the stage, straight into Adam.

"Son, shouldn't you be out there?" He was startled when Mark abruptly flung himself into his arms. "Hey now, what's all this?"

"Papa, I can't sing! I squeak. Listen, I've lost my voice."

"So you have," Adam said quietly.

Does it have to come to this? he wondered in anguish, recalling Gabriel's puzzling words. Is Mark being punished for what *I* did?

Did the archangel really think he wasn't hurting anyone?

You wanted to save Felipe, said a voice in his ear. *And he isn't hurt.*

"I can't sing," Mark said in a disbelieving whisper.

"We will be having Dr. Steve find a throat specialist." He hugged his shaking son and gave him a gentle push toward his dressing room. "Go rest now, laddie. I'll give your brother a hand."

Onstage, Felipe was staring at the mike in panic.

"Evan, I can't sing 'Scandal'!"

"Well, someone has to!"

"Aye," Adam said, picking up the other mike, "And I'm thinking it's going to be me—with a little help from you, laddie. We'll do it together."

"Papa, oh thank God. Do you know the words?"

His father just nodded.

"You two are going to do it?" Evan asked skeptically. That the older man could sing he already knew, but "Scandal"?

"I have to," Adam muttered as Felipe took up his mike. "'Tis my fault that the lad's in this mess."

Inside his dressing room, the "lad" was alternating between bouts of anger and frustration and paralyzing fear. He had tried several times to sing the words again, but only more versions of squeals and squeaks came from his otherwise normal throat. That was the surprising part, Mark suddenly realized, stopping in mid squeal.

His throat felt fine. He wasn't even hoarse.

"What the hell is going on?" the superstar cried, tossing his jacket on the sofa.

He could talk. He could even yell. He just couldn't sing.

It was as though someone didn't want him to.

Someone—like an angel?

"Papa?" Mark said in disbelief. Or another heavenly being—someone higher than his father?

Adam and Carlotta wouldn't do this. They wouldn't sacrifice one son for another. It was another being—one who wanted Adam to realize he couldn't keep breaking the rules.

"Bravo," said a soft voice behind him.

It was the young priest from Loquesta.

"Father Sanchez?" Mark blurted, puzzled at his sudden appearance. How had he even gotten backstage? Shouldn't security have stopped him? As for his odd attire -the last time he'd seen him he'd been clad in black sweats and sneakers. Now the priest was dressed in a white, glittery robe that swirled around him, and sandals were on his feet.

"No, laddie." Adam appeared in the doorway, Felipe behind him. "'Tis the archangel, Gabriel."

Gabriel made a sweeping bow, his white robe swirling around him.

"So we meet again, Mark."

The awestruck singer eyed him speechlessly as Felipe sagged onto the sofa, his boyish face devoid of color.

"Gabriel?" he whispered, swiftly crossing himself. "You're for real?"

"In the wing, so to speak." His magnificent wings unfurled before them, and Mark felt the chills invade his body. Here was an angel—the supreme being of them all.

Here also was an angel that didn't look very happy. For that matter, Adam was eying the other being belligerently. "You think taking Mark's voice away isn't hurting him?"

"Not physically."

"Are you that vindictive, Gabriel?" Adam shouted. "First Carlie and the refrigerator and dish washer, and now this?"

"Dishwasher?" Mark asked blankly.

"Aye. The kitchen is flooded."

Not really sure what the protocol was for addressing an archangel, Felipe waved a hand and waited until Gabriel turned to him.

"I don't stand on ceremony, Felipe. Ask your questions."

"I just want to know what's going on." Felipe eyed him nervously. His father and brother both looked furious.

"Has the alcohol addled your brain that much?" Mark snapped. "I told you, Papa broke some kind of ancient rule, and I'm being punished! I can't sing." His gaze swept to the archangel. "I don't care if I'm speaking out of turn or not, but banishing him and Mama from heaven seems very extreme."

"You're entitled to your opinion. And he and Carlotta knew the consequences," Gabriel said.

A disbelieving Felipe said brokenly, his voice edged with shame, "She...she really is my mother?"

"*That's* what you took from that?" cried Mark. "Didn't you hear me? They've been banished! And thanks to you, I can't sing a note." His gaze turned withering. "Suicide. You weren't raised to be a quitter!"

"Mark," Adam said, seeing Felipe's bottom lip trembling.

"No, Papa. I'm tired of handling him with kid gloves!"

The archangel said matter-of-factly, "You have doubts about Carlotta? I assure you she is your mother." He added ruefully, "And a more bull headed, feisty angel I've never met."

"I owe her an apology," said Felipe, thoroughly ashamed of how he had treated her.

Mark suddenly broke into loud, furious Spanish as he lunged at his brother, pummeling him.

"See what you've done?" Adam said to Gabriel.

"It isn't my fault that you raised Hatfield and McCoy." He raised his arm, and Carlotta, still wet from her experience with the dishwasher, appeared, blinking as she saw Gabriel.

"Why have you summoned me? I am no longer a messenger."

The archangel gestured to her squabbling sons. "But you are their mother. Do something."

Carlotta listened to the angry exchange between the two brothers. "I do not understand. Why is Marcos saying Felipe should apologize to him?"

"Because he thinks it's Felipe's fault that he can't sing," said Adam, motioning to Gabriel. "I will give you two guesses, love, whose fault it really is."

"I only need one, Adam." She shot the archangel a dark look then stepped between her two sons, somehow managing to detach Mark from his brother. Giving Felipe a swift push, she caught him off guard and he stumbled into his father.

"Bastante!" She slapped her elder son's cheek. "You are not little boys anymore, and I will not tolerate such behavior! And do not tell me who started it," she warned as Mark tried to speak.

"He did!" Felipe snapped, pressing a finger to his cut lip.

"Because you're an idiot!" As Carlotta's furious gaze swung back to him, the singer said very meekly, "Yes, Ma'am."

"And you, Felipe." She yanked her younger son forward. "Have you finally realized I am not telling you the fibs?"

"Yes, Ma'am," said a thoroughly chastened Felipe, his sheepish words echoing Mark's.

"I don't think you beat them enough when they were younger," Gabriel said, amused.

"Gabriel, your warped sense of humor does not amuse me," snapped an exasperated Carlotta.

Appalled by her words, Mark said gingerly, "Uh, Mama, do you really think you should be speaking to him like that?"

"I shall say what I please, Marcos; I am well used to his tactics. Though he has reached a new high today, soaking me with water is not funny," his mother retorted.

"I think you mean low," Felipe said, eying the arch-angel nervously. He didn't *look* angry.

"She does," said Gabriel. "Carlotta, your misuse of the English language never fails to astound me."

Carlotta looked at him witheringly before her hazel eyes slid to Mark. Grown man he might be, but his tiny mother could still make him feel like a small child, and he unconsciously moved closer to Adam. "Yes, Mama?"

"Is this your idea of taking care of Felipe, Marcos—smacking him around?"

Her contrite son muttered, "I told you I might have to beat him up a little, Mama. He's fine."

"He is bleeding. And there is no use making the eyes of a sheep. I am very disappointed." She added to her husband, "Please get out your pocket telephone, amado, and ask Mallory to pick us up. I wish to return to Ambercrest. There is still much water to be mopped."

"Pocket telephone?" Gabriel repeated.

"She...she means a cell phone..." Mark stopped in confusion, not sure how to address the archangel. He had almost called him Father Sanchez.

"Gabriel will do. And I know what a cell phone is, Mark. Unlike your parents, I am quite familiar with technology." His eyes moved to his former messenger. "Carlotta, I can send you back to Ambercrest, and I will take care of the kitchen."

"You should not have caused it in the first place," she snapped.

"You should have obeyed the rules."

"And because we didn't, you take Marcos's voice away? That is not part of the ancient laws." She pulled a somewhat damp tissue from her pocket and pressed it to Felipe's lip. "Come, Felipe. You will drive us back to Ambercrest instead."

"What about me?" her older son asked, his expression mingling panic and disbelief as he eyed Gabriel. "Are you just going to leave me like this?"

The kindly, considerate priest at Loquesta had listened to his pleas to find Adam, answered his questions; he had even held him up when he had fainted upon seeing his father. He had cared.

And yet, he had done this.

"For the moment," said the archangel.

Without warning, Mark suddenly remembered that morning in Vermont. It was the day Adam had gone missing, and the singer had pleaded with his absent father, telling him he would never sing again if Adam could only come back. It was a sacrifice he would have made willingly.

And now it seemed to be coming true.

Squaring his shoulders, Mark faced Gabriel and said flatly, "Do what you must. I don't have to sing."

"And what if it's permanent?"

"Marcos," Felipe cut in swiftly.

"If it is, I'll find something else to do. I can always go back to being a studio musician," the superstar said carelessly. He bent down and picked up his jacket. "I'm going home to my family." He brushed a kiss on his mother's cheek then left the dressing room, ignoring the others completely.

"Well, well," said Gabriel softly. "It appears you raised a fighter."

"I told you that last year," Adam retorted.

"Papa, you can't let him do this!"

"Who, laddie? Him?" Adam gestured to the archangel. "I'm afraid I'm not stopping Gabriel from doing anything. And if you're referring to your brother, your luck isn't much better. 'Tis stubborn he is—just like me," he added pointedly to Gabriel.

"Don't you two understand? Singing is his life. Marcos is just saying that!" Felipe turned to Gabriel, saying imploringly, "Please, don't take his voice away because of me. I'm not worth it."

"How very odd. He was just throwing you around the floor, and now you're defending him," the archangel said, his wings fluttering.

"Marcos and I fought worse than that when we were kids," Felipe scoffed. He gestured to his mother. "She can tell you that."

"She?" Gabriel said quietly. "I believe she has a name, Felipe."

"I do not like being referred to as *she*," said Carlotta.

"Mother," said her son, still finding it strange to say the word.

Gabriel looked at him thoughtfully. "You have a few situations of your own to worry about."

"If you're referring to suicide—"

"I am not. But you will see. As for your brother, I will consider it." His wings fluttered again and he was gone.

"What's he talking about? What situations?" Felipe asked Adam, urging them out of the room.

It was Carlotta who answered. "We do not know. But it will become apparent to you." She suddenly touched her hand to her ear. "Felipe, what is a shop vac?"

Mystified, he said, "It's a big vacuum cleaner that sucks up water. Why?"

"Gabriel says we need one."

Evasion

Adam had not exaggerated. Water was almost a foot deep in the kitchen.

Mark stood in the dining room doorway, watching Mallory push the water out the back door. He didn't question why only the kitchen was flooded, or the fact that a dishwasher couldn't be faulted for such a deluge. With the archangel, he was coming to realize that anything was possible—including losing his voice.

Mallory heard the tiny sigh he gave. "Pretty bad, isn't it? I would never have thought it possible; Miss Wings was just wondering how it worked. Then *whoosh!* Uh, I don't suppose you know why the water's only in the kitchen? Or why it seems to keep coming back?"

"Yes, but you'd never believe me, cara." He moved beside her. "Why don't you let me do that? You look exhausted."

"I am. I'm also cranky, hungry, and wet. There's no reason for both of us to be soaked." She suddenly leaned on her broom, scanning his resigned features. "You don't seem shocked at all, Mark. Were you expecting this to happen?"

"Let's just say that after the refrigerator earlier, it was par for the links, as Mama would say." He took the broom from her. "Go take a rest. I don't mind getting wet."

"The refrigerator?" Mallory echoed, turning to stare at the stainless-steel appliance.

"It was shooting ice cubes," Mark said wearily.

"Ice cubes," said his wife, thoroughly confused. "I don't suppose you'd like to explain that?"

He sighed again. "I think Gabriel believes if he gets Mama wet enough, she'll go back to heaven and take Papa with her. It's not going to work."

"Gabriel is another angel?"

"Yes."

"He did this?"

"Yes," Mark said again.

"If he caused this, why can't he clean it up? Why are we being punished?"

The superstar leaned the broom against the counter and pulled her into his arms, burying his face in her red curls. Being flooded was mild compared to what Gabriel had done to him. She was not going to know how severe the punishment really was.

"Honey, what's wrong?" Mallory felt the tremor his body gave. "If it's the kitchen, we can fix it." She drew back to look at him. "Your face, it's bruised."

"Oh." Mark touched his cheek gingerly. "That was Felipe."

"He *hit* you?" his wife said in disbelief. No wonder he was in such a strange mood; the two men were friends as well as brothers. Mallory sometimes thought they were joined at the hip.

"Only because I hit him first." Still holding his bruised cheek, he was ruefully realizing that Felipe had landed a few good ones, like when they were kids. There was a reason Adam had called them Hatfield and McCoy.

He had glimpsed Adam's face when he and Felipe had been rolling around on the dressing room floor, and his father had looked resigned, if a little amused, as though his grown sons were little boys again and still bickering.

You aren't getting them back, Gabriel, he vowed. *We're a family again.*

"*You* hit…" Mallory's skeptical words trailed away as she suddenly pointed to the floor, her hand shaking. "Mark, look!"

The water was gone. Even their clothes were dry.

A bewildered Mallory said haltingly, "Maybe he heard me."

Or me, the superstar realized. If the archangel thought dealing with one O'Hara was ruffling his wings, wait until he dealt with two more. He might not want the former messengers back.

As if on cue, the dining room door squeaked open and his parents appeared, Felipe behind them.

"We have brought the vacuum that sucks up water," Carlotta said brightly.

"Shop vac, Mama," Felipe corrected, staring around the now dry kitchen. "What happened to the water?"

Adam set down the pizza boxes and said to his elder son, "Gabriel." The archangel had said he would take care of the kitchen. Only why did the boy look angry? "Laddie, are you all right?"

"Just dandy, Papa," Mark said tersely. He touched his ear. "Papa, does he communicate the same way you do, did"—he amended—"like a…a whisper?"

"Aye," said Adam, realizing the reason for his son's attitude. "And what has he said to you?"

"Oh, just that I might not want you here," answered the singer, pouring a glass of iced tea. "And it's crap."

"Crap?" repeated Carlotta. Her confusion turned to embarrassment as Felipe leaned down and murmured an explanation for the unfamiliar word.

"Marcos!"

"Well, it is. You two can stay forever," Mark told them, and Felipe found himself nodding in agreement.

"I agree with Marcos," he said, emotion suddenly clogging his voice. "I'm sorry that I'm the reason you're here, that you can't go back."

"We want to be here, laddie," said Adam gently, putting an arm around him.

"But we have much to learn." She turned to her daughter-in-law. "Such a store Felipe took us to! So many people, wearing such odd clothing. Mallory, what is a thong?"

Mark choked on his tea. "Where on earth did you take them?"

"Walmart," his brother said, sighing. "And it was an…an experience. She wanted to ride the electric carts. Mostly she just crashed into things." He shook his head in fond exasperation. "You're a hoot, Mama."

"Mama?" said a voice behind them.

A disbelieving Rosemary stared at the newcomers, her cool green eyes taking in the fact that Carlotta had her hand through Felipe's arm, and that she was young and beautiful.

"Replace me already, sweetie?"

Replace? Felipe looked at her indignantly. "Rosemary, this is my mother."

"Right. Tell me another one."

"I do not understand," said Carlotta uncertainly. "Tell you another what?"

"She thinks I'm lying, Mama."

It was his mother's turn to look indignant. "I do not tell fibs, Rosemary."

Rosemary spun around to eye Mark. "You told me your parents were dead, remember?"

Mark set his glass down. Aware that they were treading on dangerous ground, the superstar shrugged and said casually, "They look real to me, nina."

Adam said lightly, "If you're wanting to pinch me…"

"You were here when Carlie was born," Rosemary said suddenly, "I recognize your voice now!"

"Aye," said Adam. "That I was. Did you think I didn't want to see my wee granddaughter?"

"Then why didn't I see you?" Rosemary demanded.

"Because I didn't want you to," the former messenger answered, ignoring the quelling look his son sent him. "There are times when we can't explain things, lassie, and that was one of them."

Thoroughly bewildered, Rosemary eyed them both skeptically and muttered, "I can't explain any of this! I know what I read in the interview and I know what you told me. Something isn't right." She backed away and would have fallen if Carlotta hadn't grabbed her arm.

"You must be more…" her words trailed off as she suddenly studied Rosemary, her intuitive hazel eyes concerned. "You are not feeling well, yes?"

Without thinking, Rosemary blurted, "I've been a little nauseated—wait, how the hell did you know that?"

Hell was not a word one should associate with his angelic mother, mused Felipe, stifling a grin.

"I am a good guesser," said Carlotta. "And you are quite pale."

"She's right," Felipe said, taking Rosemary's other arm hurriedly. "You probably should lie down, sweetie."

Rosemary shook free of both of them. "Since when do you care, honey? You broke up with me, remember?"

"The two of you need to mend your hedges," Carlotta said seriously, prompting Mark to say with an amused smile, "I think you mean *fences*, Mama." He gave Felipe a dark look and swiftly left the kitchen.

In the silence that followed, Rosemary said, "What's wrong with Mr. Legend? He looks mad at the world."

"No, only me," Felipe muttered, sighing heavily. "I suppose I have some hedges of my own to mend." His brother was facing the biggest crisis of his career, and he really couldn't blame Mark for his earlier actio

In the studio he found him listlessly strumming his old guitar, and silently wondered what he was supposed to say. His brother really did look like he was mad at the world.

"Marcos…"

"You really think you should leave Rosemary alone with them? Mama's liable to say anything."

"I won't be long. I-I just wanted to apologize. It *is* my fault that you're in this mess." Despair choking his voice, Felipe admitted, "I really screwed up. I've lost my confidence, I've lost Rosemary, I very nearly lost my life—all thanks to my own stupidity."

Mark laid the guitar across his lap and frowned in irritation. "Felipe, you're far from stupid."

"And you're terrified," his brother said softly, catching a quick glimpse of the panic that flared briefly in Mark's eyes.

"Wouldn't you be?"

"You still can't sing?"

"Nope, I squeak. Sometimes I squeal. Gabriel's a very funny angel," said Mark, putting a finger to his lips as Mallory came in, Carlie in her arms.

"Felipe, you might want to rescue Miss Wings. Rosemary's on the verge of twenty questions, none of which she can answer. Or Carlotta could be asking her what a thong is." As her brother-in-law sped from the studio, Mallory held the baby out to her husband.

"Apparently, I won't do. She's looking for her daddy."

"Carlita," murmured Mark, taking her. "And here I thought various grandparents had made off with you."

"Dada," said Carlie, her face puckering.

"She's fussy tonight. Maybe if you sang to her, honey?"

Damn. He hadn't even considered Carlie. His voice had calmed her on many a fussy night.

"I, uh, I would if I could, but I think Steve wants me to rest—not sing, I mean. It seems I have a frog in my throat," the superstar said, hoping she wouldn't press him. "I'll walk with her."

He had only taken a few steps when Mallory said abruptly, "Don't make the mistake of thinking he's all better, Mark. I minored in psych at college; Felipe's simply pushing it under the rug. He's trying to ignore it. He may have reconciled with Miss Wings, but that's only part of the problem. He needs to face his demons. And you really should apologize to him," she added softly, not knowing how he would take this criticism.

Mark surprised her by saying simply, "Fine, I will."

"He's going to be upset enough when he finds out she's going on a date. You will?" she echoed.

"I just said I would. I shouldn't have hit him. Mama's right; we're not kids anymore." A vision abruptly flashed across his mind—one so startling he almost dropped Carlie.

"You have to stop her, love. She can't go on a date," Mark said urgently, grabbing her hand.

Mallory stared at him. "Is this because of Felipe? *He* broke up with her, remember? What's she supposed to do, Mark, sit at home until he makes up his mind what he wants?"

He had never talked to his wife about his visions; the gift he had inherited from his Irish father was just too hard to explain. Or was it simply that he didn't want her to know—a secret that he shared with Adam and no one else?

"I can't tell you why. I doubt if you'd believe me, anyway." Ha! He wasn't even sure *he* believed the image; it just didn't seem possible. Felipe pushing a baby stroller?

But knowing how she felt about his reticence, Mark added jokingly, "Can't you activate your wonder-twin powers and talk her out of it, cara?"

Mallory leaned over and dropped a kiss on Carlie's tiny nose. "Daddy's so funny, isn't he, Carlie? He doesn't know that Aunt Rosemary is more stubborn than I am. Wonder twins!" She eyed her husband in fond exasperation. "I'll try. I think she's just trying to make Felipe jealous, anyway."

"She might force him over the edge," Mark muttered, going in search of his brother.

Felipe was in the study trying not too successfully to explain the computer to Carlotta.

"I may see anything on this?" she asked wonderingly, Adam looking over her shoulder.

"Anything. Even what's left of Loquesta," he said with a little shudder. Seeing their puzzlement, he explained how the army had turned the town into a landfill.

"But what of Elena?" Carlotta asked curiously.

"She's at an assisted-living facility in Santa Fe," Mark told them, scowling. His aunt should be living in hell after the things she had done.

"Ah," his mother said quietly. She turned around on the computer chair and took Mark's free hand in hers. "Adam has told me how she behaved, Marcos. I am truly sorry."

"Mama, there's no need for you to apologize. I just have a hard time believing that the two of you are sisters." He suddenly snickered. "It's too bad you can't… uh…pop in and scare the hell out of her; like Papa did." Remembering how Adam had paid a visit to his sister-in-law last year, Mark asked him eagerly, "Papa, you never did tell us—did she faint or just scream when she saw you?"

"Both," Adam said in satisfaction. Elena had never liked him.

"Revenge is a dish best served cold," the superstar said softly. He saw the same satisfied look on Felipe's face and said abruptly, "I'm going to borrow Felipe for a minute. Papa, please don't try to take the computer apart—I can't put it back together."

In the hallway, his brother said ruefully, "Are you beginning to feel that we're the parents and they're the kids?"

"Scary, isn't it?" Mark agreed. He shifted Carlie to his other arm and held out his hand. "I don't know what came over me earlier but I want to apologize. I shouldn't have hit you."

"You only did it because you were frightened."

Felipe knew him too well. "I'm too old to take a temper tantrum. I was blaming you for something you have no control over." Recalling Mallory's words, the superstar said earnestly, "And while you probably think this is none of my business, I think you should go see Steve. Ask him to recommend something for depression."

They both heard the cry from the study. Felipe sighed and said resignedly, "You don't think that living in the twilight zone will fix me?"

"It certainly shouldn't bore you," Mark muttered, following him back into the study.

Carlotta was staring at the screen, her eyes as wide as the proverbial saucers. "Elena," she said in a choked voice, pointing at the computer. Pushing the chair back, she flung herself into Adam's arms and cried hysterically, "She is dead! And she is going to hell for what she did to my children!"

"Oh, my," Mark said softly as Felipe crossed himself.

On the screen was a picture of Elena—in a coffin.

Rebellion

"Stay here with them," Mark said to his brother. He cast an anxious glance at his weeping mother, hoping that between Adam and Felipe they might be able to soothe her grief. He was going to confront the problem with the source.

Once in the kitchen he set Carlie in her playpen then surveyed the silent room. There must be some way to summon the archangel. Could he hear requests?

"Gabriel, if you can hear me, I'd really like to talk to you." He was halfway expecting to see him perched on one of the cabinets.

"Why are you looking on the ceiling?" The soft voice came from behind him, and Mark whirled around to see Gabriel sitting on the table, looking amused. "You have questions?"

"I wasn't sure you could hear me."

"I hear everything." The archangel gave a resigned sigh. "I did think that with Carlotta earth bound I wouldn't be dealing with her shenanigans anymore."

Of course he knew about Mama and the shopping cart. Apparently, there had been other incidents.

"She…she saw my aunt on the computer," said the singer. "I think she's dead."

"Elena." Gabriel nodded. "Yes, she died."

"Mama thinks—well, she's afraid Elena went to…to hell." *But she was evil,* his heart reminded him. *Where else would she go?* "Because of the way she treated Felipe and me."

Gabriel slid off the table and stood looking down at Carlie.

"She abandoned two children." He turned his head to glance at Mark quizzically. "I never understood why you supported her for so many years, Mark. She never acknowledged you or Felipe."

Mark gave a rueful sigh. "I suppose it was because I felt responsible for her. She didn't have anyone else." He twisted his fingers together. "No husband or children. I guess I'll have to take care of the funeral."

"Why?" Gabriel asked simply.

"Who else will? And I'm not doing it for her."

"Because of Carlotta." His wings fluttered. "You may tell your mother that Elena will be given an opportunity to repent. If she does not…"

And what were the odds of that happening? Mark wondered. His aunt never thought she had had to apologize for anything. Suddenly angry, he demanded of Gabriel, "Why did she do it? Why did she hate me so much?"

The archangel's clear brown eyes regarded him appraisingly. "She didn't." Seeing Mark about to protest his answer, Gabriel added calmly, "Every time she looked at you she saw Carlotta. She couldn't get past your resemblance to her sister. It became her way of dealing with her grief."

"By pretending I didn't exist?" Mark blurted. "And that logic doesn't apply to Felipe. He looks like…"

"Adam," Gabriel finished. "And I'm afraid Elena never cared for him; she didn't think he was good enough for Carlotta."

"Well, she was wrong," the singer snapped.

"Yes," the archangel said, turning his head away.

There had been something in the way he said that. Mark said softly, "You miss him."

"He made his choice," Gabriel said abruptly.

"You said he was good company."

"He was." He passed a hand over his face. "Look after him."

Thoroughly surprised by the request, Mark answered, "Yes, of course I will." Curious, he added, "Why aren't you telling me to look after my mother too?"

"She doesn't need it." He rolled his eyes. "In my opinion, you need protecting from *her.*" He smiled faintly. "I'm sure the people in Walmart thought so."

As Mark grinned in agreement, Gabriel stepped closer to him and touched his arm.

"You did everything you could for Elena, and then some, Mark. Carlotta knows this. But in order for her to have closure, she needs your forgiveness." His smile returned as he added, "It appears she also needs coffee—quite a lot of it."

"Coffee?" Mark asked, confused.

"Your mother is drunk." With a final chuckle, the archangel faded from view, and Mark stared after him, his mouth hanging open.

Mama drunk? Was it even possible? He had never seen her drink anything other than tea.

Hurriedly scooping up his daughter, Mark rushed back to the living room. Carlotta was no longer weeping; she was sprawled instead across Adam's lap, one arm around his neck and her hand clutching a small glass. She was also singing.

"Gabriel said she was drunk. I can't believe it," he uttered to his befuddled brother. "What on earth did you give her, Felipe?"

"Sangria," Felipe answered, shaking his head. He had never seen alcohol affect someone that quickly. "I was only trying to calm her down, Marcos. Maybe angels can't handle wine," he said slowly. Hearing her very off-key version of "Love is When I Loved You," he winced and ruefully added, "I don't think singing is one of Mama's strong suits."

"Apparently not," agreed his brother, wondering what to do. Give her coffee? Have Adam put her to bed before she woke up the rest of the household? Wish that she had chosen someone else's song to serenade her husband with?

Surprisingly, it was Felipe who urged Adam, "Papa, why don't we go in the kitchen and get Mama some coffee?"

Carlotta stopped her singing to say gaily, "I do not want coffee; I want this." She eyed her younger son suspiciously. "Felipe Sean Miguel, have you given me wine?" She shook a finger at him. "You are a bad boy."

"Yes, Ma'am." He put an arm around his giggling mother and helped Adam guide her into the kitchen.

"Dada," said Carlie.

"Daddy's confused, love," Mark said, shifting her to his other shoulder. He was startled to see Rosemary leaning against the doorway.

"What's wrong with Barbie?"

Was tonight going to be one confused episode after another? Mark wondered.   "Who?"

"The one Felipe's holding up. The one you *claim* is your mother."

Trying to keep his voice casual, the singer said flatly, "I don't claim it, Rosemary—I know it. I look just like her, in case you haven't noticed."

"Oh, I'm not saying you're not related, honey." She stepped closer to him, her hands on her hips. "She's your sister, isn't she? You and Felipe tried to cover it up."

Mark was so startled by her words that he burst into laughter.

"Rosemary, I assure you Felipe and I don't have a sister. My mother couldn't have any more children after him."

"Then why does she look like she's in high school?" Rosemary demanded.

"I don't know. Good genes, possibly," Mark said, trying to slide past her. Carlie, mistaking Rosemary for Mallory, promptly began to wail.

"That's not your mama," the superstar said darkly.

"Understand one thing, Mark. If Felipe is trying to replace me, he'll be sorry. He's not going to mess with my heart." She turned and stalked out the front door without another word.

Great. Mark stared after her, both brows lifted. Didn't Felipe have enough problems without ex-girlfriends threatening him?

"Mark, I thought you were putting her to bed." Mallory said from behind him.

"I was. Then Elena died, Felipe got Mama drunk, and Gabriel told me to look after Papa. And your dark and twisted twin threatened Felipe. You might say I got sidetracked, Mallory." He sent her a sarcastic frown as she eyed him speechlessly. "Which part do you want me to explain, cara?"

"All of it," she said, leading the way upstairs. "Miss Wings is drunk?"

"And singing—badly." He snickered. "She's going to have a beaut of a hangover in the morning."

Mallory laid Carlie in her crib and changed her diaper. "Elena is your aunt in Santa Fe? What happened to her?"

Funny, but that had never come up. "I don't know. We just saw her on the computer—dead."

"Which is why Miss Wings was drinking." Mallory nodded. "Gabriel must be missing Adam. It sounds like they are friends." She watched her husband unbuttoning his shirt. "It's hard to lose the one person you feel you can tell anything to." She saw his lip trembling and said softly, "You're feeling a little guilty, aren't you?"

"I feel like I'm living in the twilight zone," he blurted. "I don't have any control over this. I don't know what's going to happen; Gabriel is pulling the strings."

"Did you say that Rosemary *threatened* Felipe?"

"She said he wasn't going to mess with her heart; that he'd be sorry." He sighed and shook his head. "Melodramatic as usual."

"No," Mallory said flatly. "I know my sister. She means it. Felipe had better watch his step because something is going to happen."

When it did, it began with a phone call.

"Will you please give this girl your cell phone number? I don't mind being your personal secretary, but seven in the morning is too much. She woke up the baby," Mark complained, jiggling a bottle in one hand and Carlie in the other.

Felipe eyed him from his rumpled bed. "What girl?"

"The one who has called—twice." He made a face. "She says her name is Hannah."

"I don't know any Hannah. And right now I don't think I want to." He yanked the covers back over his head as he muttered, "Go away, Marcos."

Oh, no, no, no. He wasn't getting off that easily. He had some explaining to do.

"Really? So you don't know her, Felipe?" Mark sat down on the bed, carefully avoiding the dirty dishes and laundry. "That's not what she says. She told me she met you at Infinity and you're"—he broke into a southern drawl—"'cuter than a june bug on a summer night.' She's so disappointed that you haven't called." He yanked the blanket back and grinned at his brother. "Why didn't you tell me you're engaged?"

Was he dreaming this? Felipe wondered. Or was Marcos crazy?

"Engaged?" he echoed blankly, rubbing his eyes.

"As in married," said Mark. "And here I thought you didn't even know her. Did you pick a date yet? Hannah's got her heart set on Valentine's Day. I told her April Fool's Day might be appropriate."

"I'm not getting married!" Felipe blurted, now wide awake. "What the hell is going on, Marcos? It's a joke, right?" He pointed a shaking finger at him. "One of your little practical jokes that you're so fond of. You're probably in cahoots with Papa," he said darkly.

"Hey, I couldn't dream up something this good." He rose from the bed and looked at Felipe, trying not to laugh. "Oh, she's coming over, by the way. I'm sure Mama and Papa will want to meet your fiancé. " He finally gave into the laughter. "So will you, apparently."

"She's *what*?" All thoughts of sleep forgotten, Felipe scrambled from his bed, scattering dishes and laundry behind him. Hurriedly throwing on some clothes, he caught up with Mark in the hall.

"Do something! You can't just let her in here—who-ever she is!"

"You don't want to see Hannah Sue? Why, she'll be crushed."

"She's a stalker! Don't you understand? She prob-ably saw me at Infinity and cooked up this whole story. You can't seriously believe her, Marcos."

"Why not? You were getting drunk nearly every night, Felipe," Mark said, sobering. "How do I know you didn't propose? You've been acting crazy."

"If I was going to propose to anyone it would be Rosemary," Felipe retorted. "And I don't *know* any Hannah," he said flatly. "You really think I'd forget a thing like that, Marcos?" Sinking down on the bench in the hallway, he dropped his head into his hands.

"Felipe…"

"You don't believe me," he said grimly.

"Oh, good grief!" Mark reached down and laid a hand on his hunched shoulder. "You idiot, did you think I was serious?" He smirked. "Of course she's a stalker."

"Then why are you letting her come?"

"Use your head, Felipe. Suppose she goes to the press and tells them all about your so-called engagement? Or, God forbid, that she's pregnant?" As his brother started to protest, Mark held up a hand to stop him. "Felipe, I didn't say she was; I'm merely painting you a picture. One you know as well as I do," he pointed out reproachfully. "If your brain hasn't been totally fermented by alcohol, that is." His hazel eyes gleamed. "I'd rather fight this on my own turf."

"Fine, you do that. I'm going back to bed," Felipe said wearily. "Tell her you couldn't find me. Or that I'm lousy husband material. Oh, hell! Tell her whatever you please."

"Two o'clock on April Fool's Day?"

Felipe just groaned as he turned to go back to his room, his thoughts of the unknown Hannah Sue not at all kind. It was a farce—a comedy of fools—and he was the central character. A chance encounter at Infinity, if that indeed was the case, had led to her setting her cap for him.

But he couldn't remember any one with the improbable name of Hannah Sue; much less giving their number to her. He always used his cell phone.

Dammit, there had to be an explanation; some piece of the puzzle that was missing...

He stopped suddenly at the surprising sight of Carlotta staggering toward him, one hand clutching her forehead, the other pressed to the wall to steady herself. Her hair was tousled, the robe was much too big for her, and she looked totally bewildered.

"Mama?" Felipe said in disbelief, hurrying to her. He slipped his arm around her as she clutched at him desperately.

"Felipe, what is wrong with me? My head feels like little jackhammers are attacking it. And Adam is no help; he thinks it is hilarious," she said indignantly.

Her son smothered his own smile. "You're having a hangover," he said gently. And how anyone could manage that on one little drink of sangria was crazy, he mused, wondering if Gabriel had something to do with this too. "I never saw you drink before."

"I do not think I will make a habit of it." She looked at him pleadingly. "Is there anything to make it go away?"

"Coffee helps. Why didn't you just stay in bed and sleep it off?"

"I heard the phone ringing somewhere."

Ah. The mysterious Hannah, evidently. Felipe waited until they were in the kitchen and he had made both of them coffee before saying awkwardly, "Uh, there's something I have to tell you, Mama."

"Oh?" Carlotta sipped at the coffee, making a face at the unfamiliar taste. She was used to just drinking tea. "And what is that? Is it to do with Rosemary? You two have mended your hed—fences?"

Felipe smiled ruefully. "I wish." He held the sugar bowl out to her. "I screwed up everything with her and she's not very fond of me at the moment. No, this has to do with someone else—a stalker."

"Stalker," his mother repeated the strange word, and he tried to explain.

"They are like groupies, yes? I have seen them following Marcos."

"*Deranged* groupies," Felipe shuddered. "Well, this one seems to be following me. In fact, she's coming over." He bit his lip. "She…uh…she claims I proposed to her, Mama."

"And have you?"

"Good grief, no!" Felipe sputtered.

"Then perhaps this is one of the situations that Gabriel spoke of," Carlotta reminded him, and Felipe drew back to glance at her sharply, his brow puckering in thought.

Could Gabriel be responsible? Was the archangel pulling everyone's strings?

"Is he fond of practical jokes?"

"He and Adam have been known to prank"—she stumbled over the word—"each other. This does not seem like his style though."

They heard the doorbell ring and Felipe got up reluctantly. He eyed Carlotta anxiously.

"Will you be all right if I go, Mama?"

"The jackhammers have eased up a little. I think the coffee is helping." She managed a faint smile at her son. "Please tell this young lady that you were not born last night, Felipe."

At least she was in the same time period. He grinned in return and hurried off as the bell rang again.

The girl who stood on the veranda was nothing like he expected.

"Hannah?" Felipe said dubiously. He was too polite to eye her up and down, but the sight of her mousy brown hair and chipmunk cheeks convinced him that the rest of her was not much better. She wasn't pretty at all. *I must have been drunk out of my mind,* he groaned inwardly.

"You're very hard to reach, Felipe. Of course I'm Hannah," she said crisply, brushing past him into the entry. "Were you expecting someone else?"

I was expecting someone that looked halfway normal, he smothered a shudder. Why, her eyes protruded like a frog's, he realized. And he was sure she had a double chin or two. "No, that is…"

"You don't remember me, do you?" She stared at him accusingly, and he stepped back against the bench as she suddenly jabbed a finger at his chest.

"You don't! You propose to me and you don't even remember."

Where was Marcos when I needed him? Felipe thought wildly. This was his fault; he had shut off the security so she could get in here, and now he was probably somewhere laughing his ass off. He, in the meantime, was left with a girl who was a few fries short of a Happy Meal.

She could be violent for all he knew.

"Uh…my brother said we met at Infinity," he said hesitantly.

"Try again. Clubs are not my cup of tea."

But hadn't she told Marcos that?

"I, uh, I don't imagine it was at ABS?"

"Go to the head of the class. You do remember something."

Should he tell her he didn't remember a damn thing? Or was it best to play along with her and this ridiculous charade?

Taking another step backward, he said casually, "Do you work for the label?"

Hannah seemed to find this amusing. "Not likely. I'm a singer, too. Actually, an actress/singer. I left a demo tape for them to listen to."

So that was her angle. She wanted him to get the suits at the label to listen to her blasted tape. He should have known it was something like this.

So, Hannah Sue fancied herself a singer, did she?

"So you're here because you want my help with the label—not because of any engagement." He saw Mark suddenly appear in the doorway. "I think you may be confusing me with my brother. I don't have any pull at ABS."

Hannah made a slight grimace. "I don't need your help, or Mr. Legend's, and I'm here because we were supposed to go to a jewelry store today." She held up her hand. "You said you were going to replace this with a proper engagement ring."

Felipe looked at her hand and turned the color of putty.

She was wearing his signet ring.

Uncertainty

"Excuse me," Felipe muttered and fled into the kitchen.

"Hey, wait a minute," Hannah said then gave a flustered gasp as Mark came into the room.

"It seems my brother has deserted you," he drawled to the frozen girl. "Will I do? I'm Mark O'Hara."

"I…uh…I'm…"

"So you're Hannah." His arms crossed, he surveyed her calmly, still debating what was going on. Funny, she didn't sound the least like she had on the phone. She seemed to have lost her southern accent. "And you and Felipe are engaged. How and when did that happen?"

"We…uh…we…" her words fell away again, and Mark seized his opportunity.

"Or did it happen at all? Aren't you making this whole thing up, Hannah?"

Hannah seemed to shake herself, finally finding her voice.

"Of course it happened. And if I was making it up, how did I get this?" She held up her hand again and Mark saw Felipe's signet ring on her third finger.

"That's the ring I gave him when he got his diploma," the superstar muttered, shocked. "How did you get it?"

"How do you think?" Hannah retorted.

Thoroughly confused, his theory of a crazed stalker torn to shreds, Mark shook his head and told her, "I'll see what's keeping Felipe."

In the kitchen, Carlotta was trying to console her distraught son. Felipe looked up dazedly at his brother. "Marcos, I swear I've never seen that woman in my life. And I don't know how she got my ring, but I didn't give it to her!"

"Oh, I believe you." He looked at his mother and asked gently, "Are you feeling okay, Mama? Could you do something for us—a little surveillance, perhaps?"

"The jackhammers seem to be taking a break," she said as Mark looked puzzled.

"I'll explain later, Marcos," sighed Felipe. "And I don't think she understands—"

"You wish me to spy on this Hannah," Carlotta broke in.

"Yes. Just peek through the door and see what she's doing."

"She is talking on her telephone," his mother said over her shoulder.

"Probably to the person who put her up to this," Mark said, scowling.

"I wish you'd never let her in, Marcos."

"Me?" Mark stared at him. "I didn't. I thought you did, Felipe."

"Well, I didn't. Who gave her the security code?" his brother retorted. "Could someone in the band be playing a joke on me?" Felipe wondered. "A very bad joke?"

Unbeknownst to them, Mallory was looking over the banister, watching Hannah, wondering why the famous actress was in their living room.

"I should like to meet this girl," Carlotta told her sons, and Felipe snickered.

"You won't like her, Mama" he muttered, holding the kitchen door open.

Hannah looked up as the three of them entered the living room. "There you are. I was beginning to wonder. And I suppose this is your sister?" she demanded.

Before Mark could answer, Carlotta spoke quickly. "You are Hannah? I am Carlotta, their mother." She turned to her eldest son. "You might want to check on your papa. He mentioned something about the machine that plays movies. He wished to know how it works."

Mark looked at his mother in disbelief. "Papa is taking the DVD player apart? Excuse me."

"Mother?" Hannah echoed, eying Carlotta up and down. "Yeah, right. I suppose you had his brother when you were twelve. Tell me another one."

"I really do not like that expression." She glanced at Felipe. "I do not understand why people say it." Exasperated, the former messenger snapped, "I am telling you the truth. And it is no one's business how old I was when I had my sons."

"No, it isn't," Felipe agreed, putting his arm around her. He suddenly wanted to shield her from Hannah's sarcastic personality, even though she had already shown him what a tempest in a teapot her seemingly calm attitude could change to. *A tiny tornado,* he mused, trying to hide a grin. "She's very young looking."

"Young looking? Is she still in high school?" a skeptical Hannah demanded of Felipe. "She hasn't got a wrinkle in her face—not one. How can that be?"

"I believe God had something to do with it. And smoking is very bad for you. I would say drinking as well, but apparently I have a hungover, according to Felipe."

"Hangover, Mama."

"You say the two of you are engaged? How did that come about?" Carlotta gestured to the other girl's left hand. "You do not even have an engagement ring."

"We're supposed to pick one out today. That's why I'm here." She turned her attention to her alleged fiancé. "I guess you don't remember that either."

"No, I don't," Felipe said frankly. "I don't remember you, period. And I don't know how the hell you got my signet ring, but I didn't give it to you!"

"Felipe," Carlotta said, a warning in her soft voice.

"No, Mama. This is a farce. She cooked this up to get me to have the suits at ABS listen to her demo tape. I have never laid eyes on this woman in my life," he snapped angrily.

On the landing, Mallory was listening to them in vast amusement. *Oh, poor Felipe.* She shook her head as she pondered his predicament. It was too, too funny. Should she put him out of his misery or join in the joke?

"Aren't you going to introduce me to your friend, Felipe?" Mallory smiled at Hannah, and the other girl gave a tiny start.

"She's not my friend, Mallie," Felipe shot back as Carlotta said helpfully, "This is Felipe's fiancée, I think.

I am not so sure anymore. The jackhammers are back," she added with a little groan.

"Jackhammers?" Mallory echoed, concerned. Miss Wings looked very pale.

"Mama has a hangover," Felipe said curtly. "And I am not getting married!"

"I see." Mallory was having difficulty keeping from laughing. The jokesters had outdone themselves. "Tell me, Hannah, are you staying for a while?"

His unwelcome guest was looking very nervous, Felipe noticed, perplexed. And how did Mallie know her name? He certainly hadn't mentioned it.

"That's...uh...well, it's up to Felipe. He seems to think I'm here under false pretenses."

"I don't think that's true. Is it, Felipe?" Telling Hannah to make herself comfortable in the living room, Mallory nudged her sour-faced brother-in-law and Carlotta back into the kitchen.

"Oh, this is too, too funny. I knew she would do something, but I never expected this," Mallory gasped, finally giving into the laughter. Wiping her eyes, she gazed at Felipe. "That's Hannah Carson, a very accomplished actress and singer. You've been set up, Felipe."

Her outraged brother-in-law faced her with icy blue eyes. "You *know* that woman? Is that why she's so nervous—she knows you recognized her?"

"Of course I did. She's been to our old apartment enough times." As he stared at her, baffled, she went on, "You don't get it? She did warn you." She shook her head at his continued confusion. "Think, Felipe. Who's the one person who isn't here today? Who could have given her the security code? You misplaced your ring weeks ago; I remember you telling me. Who could have taken it very easily and given it to Hannah?"

A disbelieving Felipe murmured, "Rosemary—*she* did this? Why?" Pain distorted his features. "Does she hate me that much for breaking up with her?"

It was Carlotta who answered, "I should think that quite the opposite is true."

Marcos had said that revenge is a dish best served cold, and Felipe had wondered what it meant. Never, never had he figured that it would happen to him.

What had he said to Rosemary?

"You don't want to be with me now. I'm not fit to be around. Find someone who wants to enjoy life, not think it's a burden to get up in the morning -someone who has a future."

"Geez, you've got a pretty lousy opinion of me, don't you?" a furious Rosemary snapped.

"I've got a lousy opinion of *me*," he had said grimly. "And it's not getting any better."

And so it had begun, with her moving out of Ambercrest and into an apartment, and Felipe hibernating in his room, convinced that he was doing the right thing. Except for last night, they had had no real contact with each other; it was a time when he would casually ask Mallory how her twin sister was doing and secretly rejoice when she would tell him Rosemary wasn't with anyone. He had never bothered to see if she was asking about him—he told himself he really didn't have the right anymore.

"She's never said a word, has she?" he asked Mallory now, his hands trembling. "About me."

"Oh, she's said plenty. She's hurt, Felipe. She thinks you abandoned her." She was unprepared for the jubilant expression that appeared on Felipe's face. "Felipe?"

"She cares that much about me, Mallie; she went to all this trouble. I don't—"

They were interrupted by the creak of the kitchen door; a very irritated Mark saying tersely, "Your—*fiancée* is out there arguing with an angel, Felipe. Papa is calling her missy."

"Oh, dear," Carlotta murmured. She put her hand through Mallory's arm and left the kitchen.

"Why is Miss Congeniality still here? Are you picking out silver patterns?" Mark demanded.

Felipe snickered. "Oh, why not, Marcos? You don't think Hannah would make a dandy addition to the family?"

His brother eyed him incredulously. "Have you gone mad? She's arguing with Papa."

"You don't think he'll get used to her?"

"No, I do not." Both black brows lifted as he stared at Felipe. "What's going on, Felipe? You're being too calm."

"I think I could get used to the frog eyes eventually."

Mark reached out and grabbed both his arms. "I'm overjoyed you find this so funny. What do you know that I don't? Did you remember something?"

"She kind of reminds me of an egg—"

"Felipe!"

"Oh, very well. Let's go out in the living room. I think Mallie has something to tell you."

Hannah, Adam, Mallory, and Carlotta were all seated in the living room. As the brothers came in, Mallory said impishly, "This is Hannah Carson, a good friend of Rosemary's." She turned to her husband and giggled. "Hannah doesn't need to get a contract with ABS, honey. She's already under contract to Allied Artists."

"Wait a minute. Hannah Carson? You played Maria in *West Side Story* on Broadway," Mark said, studying the embarrassed actress. "You don't look anything like her."

"It's all makeup and padding," Hannah said ruefully. "Plus a very ugly wig." She shrugged. "I always wanted to do comedy."

"So you and Rosemary cooked this up together?" the superstar asked, beginning to chuckle.

"It was her idea." Hannah glanced at Felipe." She's pretty mad at you."

"So she sets me up with a bogus fiancée." He was still smiling that lopsided grin. "She's outdone herself." He leaned over and lightly touched her arm. "On the off chance that I can keep from throttling her, just where is Rosemary? I assume she is still in the country?"

"Probably at her apartment." Hannah slipped his ring from her finger and held it out to him. "She was waiting to hear from me."

"Well, she's going to hear from someone—namely me!" He snickered.

"Tell her I offered Hannah my congratulations, or do I mean condolences?" Mark added, smiling at Hannah.

The actress gave a little start when Felipe's bright blue eyes fastened on her. She found herself wondering just why he and Rosemary had broken up; her friend hadn't really said anything about it beyond the fact that she wanted to teach Felipe a lesson. "He's not gonna play with my heart and just leave me in the lurch," was how she had put it to Hannah. She had only gone along with the practical joke because she was curious about the O'Haras, Felipe in particular. He was so much in his older brother's shadow that she wondered what he was really like.

For all his bitterness and anger, she had glimpsed sadness in those eyes.

"Anyone who gets me should be condoled," Felipe muttered, searching for his phone. Not finding it, he looked at Adam in fond exasperation. "Papa, hand it over. I know you have my phone."

Sheepishly smiling, Adam told him, "I was taking pictures of Carlie, laddie. Aye, 'tis a miracle that something so tiny can be a camera."

"Better upgrade him, Marcos. He'll be wanting one that talks to him next," said Felipe.

A wide-eyed Adam said wonderingly, "There is such a thing—a phone that actually talks?"

"Yes, her name is Siri. And I don't think she would like being taken apart, Papa." Seeing Hannah's expression and the question hovering on her lips, the superstar said quickly, "My parents have lived in a…a retreat for many years, Hannah. They're not too familiar with modern technology."

Heaven—a retreat? Felipe couldn't help grinning at his brother's words as he clicked on Rosemary's number. *Well, why not? It was a paradise, after all.*

"Sweetie, you should be here. You're missing all the fun," he said when she answered.

"So you've met Hannah? I do think you could have told me you were engaged, Felipe." She heaved a heavy sigh. "First Barbie, now Hannah. I'm crushed, I tell you."

"You're the most uncrushable—wait, who's Barbie?" Felipe echoed, looking at Mark blankly. His brother motioned to Carlotta, and a puzzled Felipe said, "Why are you calling my mother Barbie?"

"She reminds me of a doll I used to have. She never aged either," Rosemary said tartly.

Sometime soon, he feared he would have to explain about Adam and Carlotta, even if it defied rational thinking. *Ha! More like something the Twilight Zone writers would dream up,* he mused after hanging up. Felipe doubted she would even believe him; she was not the romantic daydreamer like Mallory. Rosemary was very much like him—a realist.

She would want proof.

"Laddie?" Adam said worriedly, wondering about the boy's pensive expression.

"She's not going to believe me," he muttered, relieved that Hannah had gone and they could talk openly. "There are times *I* don't believe it, and I have proof."

He was in a daze, Mark realized, dropping down beside him on the sofa.

"You wanna come back to this planet, hermanito?"

"How do I explain this, Marcos?" He eyed their parents. "Is this one of the situations Gabriel was referring to? I have to tell Rosemary about you two. What do I say? That you used to be angels and now you *aren't*? Oh yeah, she'll buy that."

"It is the truth," Carlotta said gravely.

"Then what happened to your wings?" He flung up his hands. "On TV angels glow."

Adam said, "But why do you have to tell her now, laddie?"

It was Carlotta who said firmly, "Because he must, amado." Her beautiful hazel eyes skipped to her younger son. "I may not be a messenger anymore, but I still know things. The inside mud, you could say."

"Dirt, Mama," Felipe said, grinning. "Spill it...I mean, tell me."

"I cannot spill it. But it is one of the situations Gabriel was talking about, and you should know quite soon."

"But when I asked you before, you said you didn't know," Felipe reminded her.

"I didn't *then*," Carlotta said mysteriously.

Her puzzled husband said, "But Gabriel has not confided in you, Carlie."

"He didn't have to," the serenely smiling former messenger said. She turned back to Felipe. "You should tell Rosemary about us as soon as possible, Felipe. I wish that we could glow for her but—"

"Did you have wings?" Mark asked abruptly, suddenly curious.

"Of course. Your papa had magnificent ones," Carlotta answered.

"Don't you miss them?" Felipe was still feeling very guilty.

It was his father who said firmly. "Not as much as we would miss *you* and our grand..." his words trailed off as he suddenly eyed his wife, and a slight smile curved his lips. "Oh!" he said softly.

Angel speak? Felipe wondered, eying his parents warily.

Apparently so. "We are not going to spill it," Carlotta told him. "Talk to Rosemary."

"Aye. Mend your fences, laddie," Adam said, still smiling.

He just hoped the "fences" hadn't been torn down, a rueful Felipe mused.

But as time passed, it seemed that Rosemary had gone from pranking him to outright avoidance. She wasn't at Ambercrest, she wasn't at her apartment, and his phone calls went unanswered. He had even had Mark call from his phone to no avail. Rosemary seemed to have disappeared.

"Where is she?" Felipe demanded of his sister-in-law. "I know she told you, Mallie, you're the one person she would tell. Did it ever occur to her that I might be worried?"

"She's fine, Felipe. She just wants some time to herself."

"Great—another person who doesn't need me," he muttered, not realizing that Mallory had overheard his plaintive words. She stared after him as he stormed off, finally realizing the demon that drove her brother-in-law. So simple, really.

She left Carlie with her assorted grandparents and drove off to Hannah's apartment.

"I don't care if you're still pissed off at him; you're coming back to the house with me," she told her twin.

"Why should I?" Rosemary, pale and unsmiling, retorted.

"Because I'm worried about Felipe. Do you know why Adam and Carlotta are here, Rosemary? It wasn't just to see Carlie. Felipe's tried to commit suicide... twice." As her sister's mouth sagged open, Mallory said flatly, "Next time he might do it."

Stupefaction

Were they running a hotel? Felipe couldn't remember the house ever having this many people in it. The Kaplans were in the living room with Carlie; Rhythm Nation were jamming in the studio; Rosemary, who surprisingly, had moved back in, was in her room; Marcos was fussing over something in the kitchen; and his parents, when last seen, were in the study, agog over a movie and microwaved popcorn.

That left only Mallie, who seemed to have disappeared. Or so he thought.

"Felipe!" The urgent whisper came from behind him, and Felipe spun around to see Mallory beckoning to him from a closet.

"You hiding from someone, sweetie?"

"It doesn't do any good. They always find me. Do you know where Mark is?"

"Probably trying to put the microwave back together. Papa wanted to know how it makes popcorn. Do you want me to get him?"

"Just tell him to come to the linen closet," Mallory said quickly.

"The linen closet," Felipe echoed dubiously.

Could she do this? Could she be as brazen as Rosemary?

"Yes. There's no other place to hide. And don't let anyone hear you!"

Mallie holding meetings in a closet, Rosemary having a pity party in her room—what next? Felipe wondered, finding his brother staring at a cookbook.

"You're supposed to go to the closet."

"Que?" the startled singer asked, looking at him blankly.

"Mallie. Go to the linen closet. She didn't say why."

Mark gave his brother a perplexed look, sighed, and went up the back stairs. He paused in front of the closet, wondering just where Mallory was, when the door suddenly opened and she pulled him inside before he could say a word. In complete darkness, Mark started to say her name, but her lips were suddenly on his and he completely forgot the dinner he was supposed to be making.

"Why, Mrs. O'Hara, what's gotten into you?"

"You, I hope." Her hands were unbuttoning his shirt. "I'm trying to seduce you. Why aren't you taking your clothes off? We haven't much time."

"So we're having a quickie in the closet?" His surprised body was already noting that Mallory had shed her sundress, and it really didn't matter where they were.

"They'll find us anywhere else. And what's wrong with the closet?"

Well, there wasn't as much room as she had thought. Her foot caught the edge of a pile of laundry and sheets, towels, and everything else cascaded down on them.

"Mark?"

Her husband was laughing as more laundry fell. "I'm sorry, I'm just glad it isn't the cleaning supplies." He pulled her onto his lap, still chuckling. "I don't think this is going to work, amada," he said gently. "You have no idea how much I wish it would"—*how much he wanted her,* Mark thought longingly—"but it's getting a little dangerous. And this is the biggest closet."

A very frustrated Mallory said, "It's been two weeks, Mark. The house is full of people. Your parents, my folks, Rosemary, Felipe, and now the band shows up. I think we're running a bed and breakfast." As an idea struck her, she added hopefully, "That's it! Why couldn't we run away? Just one night at a hotel." She let her fingers trail over his chest. "One night, Mark, away from everyone."

"Uh…would an apartment do? ABS keeps one available for me at the complex."

"They do? You never told me."

I never told you I can't sing anymore either, a very guilty Mark thought ruefully. He had tried telling himself that he didn't want her to worry, but he had a very bad feeling that his wife would be calling him far worse names than patoot when she found out.

It was strange, really, that no one had connected the dots. It was the longest break he had ever had. No performances, no sessions, and no one had said a word. Divine intervention, perhaps?

"I've never used it that much." He helped her straighten up the closet and pull her dress on. "I'll make the arrangements then."

Downstairs, the quiet kitchen Mark had left such a short time before was in chaos. Carlie was crying in her highchair; Rosemary was hunched over the garbage can, vomiting, Felipe vainly trying to help her; and in the corner, Gabriel, looking perplexedly at the screaming baby.

Picking up her wailing daughter, Mallory whispered to Mark, "Who is that?"

"Gabriel," he said simply.

As Mallory stared in fascination at the white-gowned being, Rosemary gave a shuddering hiccup and told her sister, "Mallie, I was going to feed her and then I barely made it to the can."

"You've been doing that a lot recently," Mark said, his hazel eyes reflecting on his sister-in-law's unorthodox behavior of late—nausea, mood swings, sleeping more than usual. She hadn't even gone to Infinity in weeks. She didn't seem to be smoking either.

And then he knew. Just as Carlotta had noticed, so had he.

"I...uh...I guess it—I mean I haven't been eating right," Rosemary muttered, wiping her face.

"It was not something you ate," said Gabriel.

"Who is this person?" She eyed him suspiciously. "Are you a new member of Rhythm Nation?"

Gabriel's glittery robes swirled around him as he stepped closer to Rosemary. "No, but I am rather proficient at the harp." He glanced from Mark and Mallory to the puzzled Felipe.

"You know, Mark?"

"Yes, sir."

"And Mallory knows what's wrong as well."

Mallory did know. She had had morning sickness the first three months of her pregnancy. She glanced at the unsuspecting Felipe, not knowing whether she should rejoice or worry. Was this God's way of dealing with Felipe's particular demon? Was he taking matters into his own hands and sending Gabriel to pull the strings? Felipe was going to be a father. She nodded, unable to take her eyes off the magnificent creature. There was such a sense of awe and confidence about him.

"I...I don't know what to call you," she blurted finally.

"Gabriel will do." He turned back to her sister. "Don't you think you should tell Felipe?"

"Tell me what?" Felipe asked, bewildered by the exchange.

"Nothing!" snapped Rosemary. "I don't think you need to know about my stomach flu."

"He does need to know that you're pregnant," Mark said abruptly. As Felipe's knees buckled under him, his brother quickly caught him and pushed him onto a chair.

"Pregnant?" His voice a mere squeak, his disbelieving eyes slid from Rosemary's ashen face to Gabriel's amused one. "But we—I mean, how? When?"

"Ask him!" Rosemary waved a hand at the oddly dressed stranger.

"In about eight months, I should say," said Gabriel.

"Should I be getting brandy?" Mark gazed at his brother's wan face worriedly. He wasn't eating right either, wasn't even thinking that clearly yet, and now to hear news like this?

"He's not going to faint," the archangel said calmly as Mallory stared at him curiously. So magnificently arrogant; the highest angel of them all.

"You're the angel of communication," she blurted, suddenly remembering a book she had read.

"I am, indeed."

"Angel?" Rosemary squeaked as the door burst open and Adam came in. He stopped short when he saw Gabriel.

"So you're back. Still hoping I'll change my mind, Gabriel?"

"The deadline is long past, Adam. I'm here out of curiosity, nothing more."

"So be it. I only came in to make more popcorn in the silver box."

"It's a microwave, Adam! If you're going to live in this time, at least learn the terminology," the archangel snapped.

Surprisingly, it was Felipe who stirred from his befuddled state to say suddenly, "I...I can teach you, Papa. Both of you." He added dazedly, "And Papa, you're going to have another grandchild."

As Adam's gaze skipped from him to Mark, the singer motioned to his brother. "Not me, Papa. This one's McCoy's."

"I'm having a baby," Felipe blurted.

"*I'm* having it, you patoot!" Rosemary snapped before turning to stare at Gabriel. "And I would really like to know who or what you are."

For answer, Gabriel abruptly unfurled his magnificent wings. Rosemary shrieked and sagged into a chair.

"The archangel Gabriel at your service." He saw her eyelids flutter and announced, "This one is going to faint."

Felipe roused himself from his confusion and hurriedly moved to her side, putting his arms around her as Rosemary suddenly slumped against him.

"Showoff," Adam muttered.

"She asked." He looked around the spacious kitchen and added, "Why isn't Carlotta in here insulting me?"

"She's watching a video of Mark on television." He suddenly wagged a finger. "See? I know what a video is now, Gabriel."

"Bravo," the archangel said drily. "Does she know how to fast forward the commercials?"

The former messenger said blankly, "Fast forward what?"

"Never mind, Adam." He looked at Felipe. "Good luck teaching him. How-to books and visual aids might help."

"Speaking of my son." Adam cleared his throat. All traces of his brogue vanished as he said flatly, "Don't you have some unfinished business with him, Gabriel?"

"I haven't decided."

Adam smiled sweetly. "Unless you want me to sic Carlie on you?"

"Oh, very well. Mark, come here," Gabriel ordered.

Rosemary's green eyes were finally open. Still cuddled against Felipe, she watched in frightened disbelief and awe as her brother-in-law moved slowly toward the winged creature.

"What are you doing?" Mallory burst out as the archangel pressed his hand to Mark's throat.

"Giving him his voice back."

"You can't *sing*?"

Well, he was in for it now. He sighed at his wife's angry words then shivered suddenly as a swirling tide of energy seemed to flow from Gabriel.

"He can now." The archangel's fingers dropped to the superstar's shoulder. "I meant what I said before, Mark. You have a rare gift from the Heavenly Father. You touch souls," he said softly. "Though I suspect Adam thinks he had something to do with it." He glanced at his former messenger. "This was one of your few failures. You're a prime example why I don't send messengers to save family members. You were too close; you couldn't see that what Felipe needed was responsibility. He wants to take care of someone. Now he has that again. You might say he was born to be a father," he said wryly. Eying Rosemary, he added ruefully, "You put me in mind of your future mother-in-law—a free spirit, if I ever saw one." Gabriel said softly, "Carlotta never needed wings to fly."

Was he saying good-bye? Mark wondered, tears glinting in his eyes at the very apt description of his mother.

"Mother-in-law?" Rosemary echoed, looking perplexed. "But we're not getting married."

"Wanna bet?" the archangel retorted. His brown eyes moved to Felipe and he took his hand between both of his. "You need to believe in yourself." The swirling energy enveloped the dumbstruck Felipe. "Suicide isn't the answer. As your father told you last year, your story is just beginning." His robes flowed around him as he stepped close to Adam and embraced him.

"You made the right decision," he said softly as his speechless friend nodded. "They're going to need you, Adam."

"Will I be seeing you again?" Adam finally found his voice.

Gabriel smiled mysteriously as he put both hands on the former messenger's cheeks.

"You might not need to, but we'll see." His wings fluttered and he was gone. In the emptiness that followed his departure silence reigned, broken only when Carlotta suddenly came in the kitchen.

"Adam, you have forgotten our popcorn."

Suddenly, all of them seemed to be talking at once, even Carlie.

"Coming, my love!"

"Dada!" wailed the baby, looking for her father.

Mark hurriedly picked her up, telling his mother, "Mama, I can sing again, I think."

"You patoot! You couldn't be bothered telling me something that important?"

"Mama, we're having a baby! We're pregnant. I mean, Rosemary is."

"He had wings—real wings," Rosemary whispered, clutching Felipe's hand.

Carlotta heard her awestruck words and gazed at Adam searchingly. "Gabriel?" As her husband nodded, she sighed and added solemnly. "The dice is cast then. He is not coming back."

"You mean die, my love." He looked at her anxiously. "Are you all right with that, Carlie? That he is probably not returning?"

"Of course, Adam. It was my decision, you remember?" Her hazel eyes swept over the befuddled Rosemary. "And we have much to celebrate, amado. A new grandchild…"

"Which you already knew about," Mark said, still eying his wife nervously. There were too many sharp objects at hand for his liking.

"I am sure you saw the signs as well, Marcos." She looked at her eldest son closely. "You are relieved that Gabriel stopped being childish and came to his senses?"

Relieved? He was overjoyed. Seeing Carlotta put her hand to her ear, Mark knew she was listening to the archangel. "Mama? What's he saying?"

"Something about crap." She looked pointedly at the superstar and said severely, "And that you should have told Mallory the truth."

"Yes, he should! It's like the nervous breakdown all over again!" Her eyes flashed emerald fire. "That's why you weren't singing to Carlie—you *couldn't*. Why do you keep shutting me out, Mark? Why couldn't you have just told me what happened?"

His own temper beginning to fray, Mark retorted, "What would you have done, Mallory? Worry with me? Hold my hand? I didn't tell you because I was afraid it might be permanent!"

Carlie heard her father's angry voice and promptly burst into tears.

"Oh, damn," muttered the singer, feeling miserable that he had upset her. Whirling around, he by passed Carlotta's waiting arms and thrust Carlie at Felipe.

"Here. You need the practice." His startled brother gazed at Carlie gingerly. "If she keeps crying just sing to her. Mallory seems to think that's all I'm good for."

"That is not true!" But Mark paid no attention to her quick denial; he had already stalked out of the kitchen, intent on reaching the sanctuary of his studio.

Back in the kitchen, Felipe eyed Carlie with a type of fascinated wonder. Always having refused to hold her in the past, he wasn't quite sure what to do with her. She had stopped crying and seemed content to snuggle in his arms, her small green eyes focused on him puzzledly.

"She's staring at me," he said softly.

His soon-to-be fiancée said, "You've never been around a baby before, I can see. Sweetie, you've got a lot to learn. But first"—Rosemary looked up at her angry twin—"Mallie, for God's sake, stop being a drama queen. He's not shutting you out. You're going to have to realize that he's not used to confiding in people."

"Not even me, sometimes," Felipe said gravely.

"But I'm his *wife*!"

"And he loves you," Rosemary insisted. "Go talk to him. We can take care of Carlie."

"Da," said Carlie, reaching up a small hand to Felipe.

"See? She's fine. When she pees on Felipe I'll show him what a diaper is." After Mallory very reluctantly left the kitchen, Rosemary turned to the unusual couple that would soon be her in-laws.

"All right, you two. What gives?"

"Gives?" Adam echoed, glancing at his son.

"She wants to know what's going on." Settling Carlie on his lap, Felipe said slowly, "Sweetie, I think there's something I better tell you."

"About Ken and Barbie here? Or that person with the wings?" Still in total disbelief over what she had seen, Rosemary said haltingly, "I know it had to be a costume, but they looked like real *wings*. And then he just disappeared. *Poof!* I mean, where did he go?"

"Back to heaven, I guess," Felipe said calmly as his new fiancée gasped.

"Heaven?" she stammered.

"Well, he is the archangel Gabriel. And my parents were two of his messengers. That's why they look so young," he said, and Carlotta nodded.

"It is good that you are not speaking the fibs, amado. Since Rosemary is going to be a member of our family she needs to know the truth."

"*Angels?* Both of you?" she whispered, trembling. "But that means…that you *died*."

"Yes," Adam said quietly. "The factory I worked in blew up, and Carlie—"

"I had cancer," his wife announced. "Marcos and Felipe were still so young and I felt very badly about leaving them, but I wanted to be with Adam," Carlotta said wistfully.

"But I wasn't there."

"Not for a very long time."

"I searched so long for her. I had almost given up." Adam smiled affectionately. "I knew there was something I had to do, but I was not thinking I had to save my own son to find her."

"I had to bring Marcos and Mallory together." Carlotta announced. "They did not want to cooperate."

"And I had to keep them together." His smile turned rueful. "T'was not easy."

"But how did the two of you finally hook up?" Rosemary asked.

"Ah. That was the funny thing. I kept hearing words in my mind 'four souls will suffer,' and I wasn't knowing what they meant."

"I heard the same words." Carlotta nodded in agreement.

"So when Mallory was telling me the same four words, I knew something was happening. I knew another messenger was communicating with the lass." Tears glistening in his bright-blue eyes, he went on, "I did not dream it was my Carlie."

"Amado," Carlotta whispered, laying her head on his shoulder.

"Arun m'chroi," murmured Adam in return.

Felipe and Rosemary looked away in embarrass-ment, but baby Carlie chose that moment to demand attention. After changing her, Rosemary asked curi-ously, "My folks said you disappeared from the farm; is that when you found each other again?"

"Aye. Gabriel had summoned me back—I had to go. There will be no arguing with him when his mind's made up; I tried. I didn't wish to leave you, laddie." He looked at his younger son. "But after I talked to the lass, there was no keeping me there."

"I thought I'd never see you again, Papa," Felipe said haltingly. He reached over and pressed his mother's hand. "And I never dreamed I'd see you, Mama."

"I never left you, Felipe." Her smile faltered as a tear slid down her cheek. "Even when Elena abandoned the two of you."

"Elena?" Rosemary repeated.

"My aunt," Felipe said witheringly.

Sensing that the unknown Elena was not something he wished to discuss, Rosemary said quickly, "So you're together again and now you're here. But you don't have wings. Not like the dude that vanished." She felt herself shivering. "They were awesome." Suddenly touching her ear, she turned startled eyes to Felipe.

"What's wrong, sweetie?"

"A voice—I think it said thank you."

"Ah. Gabriel is communicating with you." Carlotta looked at her husband and said fondly, "I think Adam's were just as magnificent."

"Aye. They were grand."

"But you don't have them now," said Rosemary, mystified. How could you just lose *wings*?

"No, not anymore. We are earthbound now."

"Why?"

"We made a choice," Carlotta said simply.

"That's not quite true, Mama." Still feeling enormously guilty for his part in their decision, Felipe said brokenly, "Yes, they made a choice, but it was because of *me*, Rosemary. They knew I wanted to kill myself."

Even though Mallie had mentioned it, Rosemary felt sick inside. She had not seen the signs either. Just like his brother, he was prone to keeping things to himself, denying any kind of help.

"I didn't think I was worthy of you…of anyone. But they saw"—he nodded to his parents—"and they came when they weren't supposed to. They broke some kind of law. And so they were banished." His voice broke and Felipe buried his face in Carlie's red curls.

"Laddie," said Adam helplessly, unsure how to comfort him.

"For that I will always feel guilty…and grateful."

"Wait a minute." Rosemary looked at them indignantly. "You two came back to help Felipe, and Mr. High-and-Mighty Archangel sends you packing? All because you wanted to help your son? He has a nerve!"

As her in-laws-to-be smiled gratefully, Rosemary said tartly, "Now he's saying something about rules."

"Rules!" sniffed Carlotta, her hazel eyes narrowing. "Him and his ancient laws. Some of them are ridiculous. And then he childishly takes Marcos's voice away because he is in a snot."

"Snit, my love."

"Gracious. Your poor brother—onstage and he could not sing. He must have been terrified," she told Felipe, who nodded ruefully.

"Terrified, bewildered, helpless—not words I would use to describe Marcos. He didn't know what to do. Papa and I had to finish 'Scandal' for him."

"I didn't know you could sing too," said his impressed fiancée.

"I don't do it all that often," Felipe admitted. He had a feeling he would be doing it a lot more, if Gabriel's prophecy proved correct. *Just not "Scandal" again,* he prayed. *That was Marcos' song.*

In the studio, a very spirited version of that song was going on as Mark had discovered his voice was indeed back and better than ever. He was so enthralled in the impromptu jam session that he had completely forgotten the argument with his wife.

To Mallory, watching and listening from the doorway, it was a bittersweet moment. She knew she should still be angry, knew that Rosemary was right—that her very private husband would always keep certain things from her. But to hear him sing again? She was shivering.

"Four souls will suffer," the quiet voice said behind her, and she turned to see Gabriel leaning against Felipe's piano, watching her. "Did you know, Mallory? You were one of the souls."

Mallory nodded, still mesmerized by his appearance. "I thought you had gone, G-Gabriel."

"It occurred to me that I hadn't spoken to you." He crossed his arms and said musingly, "The four of you present a multitude of differences. Carlotta is a free spirit, a gypsy who never cared where I sent her; Adam, brilliant but naive, thinking he could help everyone. Mark is very much like his father but he doesn't have Adam's innocence. Your husband had to grow up much too quickly," Gabriel said ruefully. "His is the old soul. He will never change, and I don't believe you really want him to. That is whom you fell in love with."

"And me?" she blurted.

"Ah. Where your twin sister is a realist, you are a complete dreamer—a romantic." He took her hand in his. "You want to live in a fantasy world. But that world does not take courage—*this* one does."

He bowed his head over their clasped hands "A great deal of courage," he added softly. "I'm glad you have it, Mallory."

Gabriel and his odd, flowing energy disappeared as silently as they had come, leaving Mallory to puzzle over his enigmatic words. Courage? It didn't make sense. Did she have any? And why would he bring it up now?

"Are you trying to tell me something?" she found herself whispering.

But there were no words in her ear or a sign that Gabriel had even heard her. She felt the strange energy from the archangel overwhelm her, and her anger fell away as quickly as it had come. It was suddenly far more important that she see Mark, and she burst into the studio.

The superstar stopped in mid word as Mallory held out her hand to him.

"Gabriel's right—you are an old soul and I don't want you to change." She took a deep breath, trying not to notice the very interested expressions of the band, and said hurriedly, "I just wish you would talk to me more." The familiar chemistry between them both tingled and soothed her as Mark closed his fingers around hers.

So the archangel had been talking to his wife as well. "Done," Mark said softly, wondering just what else Gabriel had said. She didn't even look angry. And what was an "old soul?" He had never heard the expression before. "Are we going back to the closet?" he asked hopefully. Maybe they could rearrange the towels and cleaning supplies.

Mallory went on as though she hadn't heard him. "I am not a drama queen, no matter what my sister says. And for your information, yes, I think your singing is important, but that's because I love your voice. Is there something wrong with that?" she demanded, her jade-green eyes flashing.

"I—"

"You might want to be careful how you answer that, amigo," Ryan said, trying not to smile.

"No, not at all," said Mark hastily.

"Good. Now we can go to the closet."

"Yes, ma'am," said the superstar, grinning.

Mallory stopped in front of her parents and told them, "I think Rosemary and Felipe have something to tell you."

In the kitchen, Felipe was saying firmly, "We're getting married as soon as possible."

"Geez, you really know how to be romantic, don't you?" Rosemary snapped. "Did it ever occur to you to *ask* me, you patoot? And on the very remote chance I might say yes, I want a ring." She added defiantly, "Not your signet ring either."

"Felipe, she should have a diamond," Carlotta told her son.

"See? Barbie understands," Rosemary said triumphantly.

"Her name isn't Barbie!" her frustrated fiance snapped.

"Mallory calls me Miss Wings," said Carlotta helpfully.

"Fine, we will go shopping for a diamond," Felipe said, pushing back his chair. He handed Carlie to Adam and stood looking at his stubborn fiancée. "Then we'll find a justice of the peace."

Rosemary got to her feet, her own green eyes flashing dangerously. "No, we won't! Not if you're gonna yell at me. No man is ever gonna yell at me again, Felipe O'Hara." She stalked from the kitchen without a backward glance, nearly running into her parents.

"Honey, what's wrong?" Mary said worriedly.

"Him!" She pointed at Felipe. "He wants to get married!"

Not exactly sure why his daughter was so angry, Lucas said, chuckling, "The nerve of him."

"Sweetheart, I think that's wonderful!" Mary told her happily.

"I wouldn't marry him if he was the last man on earth!"

Aggravation

"She is the most bull-headed, frustrating woman I've ever met!" Felipe snapped.

"Adam?"

"Yes, my love?"

"We are back to square one." Carlotta said as her son erupted into a stream of Spanish. As the Kaplans and Adam looked from Felipe to her, she sighed and told them, "It is better that I do not translate. He is being very colorful."

"I'm not sure I blame him. Son," Lucas said gingerly. "Don't you think you'd better go after her?"

"She'll just call me a patoot again," Felipe muttered.

"I am not sure what *patoot* means, but Rosemary is right; you were certainly not being romantic. You should have proposed—like your papa did with me," Carlotta said seriously, the memory twinkling in her eyes.

"Mama, I would have, but have you forgotten there's no time?" He turned to the Kaplans. "I really didn't want to tell you like this, but Rosemary is pregnant."

"So that's what Mallie meant," Mary said, smiling. "She knew, of course."

"Apparently everyone knew—except for me," muttered Felipe.

"Gabriel told him," Carlotta said brightly.

"Carlie," said Adam, a warning in his voice as Mary and Lucas eyed his wife blankly.

"Gabriel?" repeated Mary.

Felipe said swiftly, "Never mind Gabriel. Mama, why don't you and Papa take baby Carlie upstairs and change her?"

"But she is not wet," his mother pointed out. "Rosemary changed her, remember?" She gazed at her younger son and suddenly wagged a finger at him. "You are trying to get rid of me, yes? I think you would do better to do what Lucas suggests and go after Rosemary." Carlotta shook her head and said to the Kaplans, "He really does love her; he just does not know how to show it properly."

"Like Marcos, I suppose," Felipe said sarcastically. "Flowers and candy and everything in between, even a song. Well, I am *not* my brother!" He reached out abruptly and took Carlie from his father. "Let's go, lovey. You're the only one who isn't judging me."

"Da," said Carlie, cooing at him.

The two of them disappeared through the kitchen doorway as a very shocked Carlotta said in protest, "But I was not comparing you to Marcos! You are not even remotely like him."

Adam added, "He's not like me, either. I certainly didn't tell you we were getting married."

"No, but you insisted on getting me an emerald," Carlotta reminded him. "You did not even consider that I might not like emeralds. I actually wanted a diamond," she added abruptly, surprising her husband with this unexpected admission.

"Am I really hearing this? You want a *diamond*?" Adam sputtered indignantly. She couldn't have told him this years ago? "I thought you liked emeralds."

"You did not ask me!" Carlotta retorted, springing to her feet.

"Fine. We'll get you a diamond then!" Adam all but shouted at her.

"In Rosemary's words, 'not if you were the last man on heaven or earth'!" Carlotta furiously flung the words at him before stalking up the back stairs. A befuddled and angry Adam slumped into a chair as the Kaplans looked on sympathetically.

"Does Mark have any whiskey in the house?" Lucas asked. "I think you could use a drink."

"He has Jameson. T'is good Irish whiskey," Adam answered, trying not to show how much the out-of-the-blue argument had upset his composure. It had been a very long time since they had argued—so long he could barely remember. "I could use the whole bottle, Lucas."

"I don't think getting drunk is going to help the situation, Lucas," Mary objected. "He needs to talk to Carlotta."

"There will be no talking to her now. She will be throwing things at me and not just words."

"What would you have him do, Mary? Apologize for something that happened years ago? Why should he?" Lucas retorted, putting a friendly hand on the other man's shoulder.

"Because he made a mistake! It's the right thing to do," Mary snapped at him.

"That's *your* opinion!" her husband shot back. "Adam was just trying to please her."

"Then he should have found out if she liked emeralds!"

In the living room, Felipe heard the angry voices and sighed.

"Close your ears, lovey," he said as he sat down before his piano and settled Carlie on his lap. "They're using language you shouldn't hear. We'll just ignore them."

"Ga!" shrieked Carlie, bringing both hands down on the keys.

A short time later Mark stood in the entry staring at his brother.

"Hermanito, what's going on?"

"We're playing the piano," Felipe said briefly, not even turning around.

"What kind of madhouse is this? The Kaplans are yelling at each other in the kitchen, Mama and Papa are fighting upstairs, Rosemary is in her room crying, and here you are giving my daughter a piano lesson."

"She likes the noise. Don't you, lovey?" said Felipe.

Lovey? Mark echoed, wondering what had gotten into him. "Felipe…"

"You want to know what's going on? I told Rosemary we were getting married. Apparently, that's not the way to do it." He swiveled on the piano bench to frown at his perplexed brother. "That's not the way *you* do it."

"What the hell do I have to do with it?"

"You're a romantic, I'm not, according to the assorted women in this family. And they were quite vocal about it." Scowling, he said bitterly, "I'm just a man who wants to get married and give his child a name. And I would like to know what's wrong with that!"

"Not a thing," Mark said hastily, wincing as Carlie banged more keys.

"Er...maybe you should try *asking* her," he ventured, unsure how to phase it.

"Maybe. She'll probably just yell at me again. And I was not going to give her my signet ring as an engagement ring," Felipe said furiously.

"Ga," said Carlie, blowing bubbles at him.

"Yes, lovey, whatever you say."

"Of course you weren't." Totally confused by this new version of Felipe, Mark said cautiously, "I don't suppose you know why Mama and Papa are arguing?"

"Mama wanted a diamond—she got an emerald instead."

"Emerald?" Mark echoed blankly. "You mean the one I gave Mallory? *That* emerald?"

"Yep. She didn't like it. She wants a diamond."

"Uh-huh. And the Kaplans?"

"Mary doesn't approve of using whiskey as anger therapy; Lucas does. Papa and he are probably going to get drunk—I may join them," Felipe said glumly.

"Fine, you do that. If you and the princess are done making noise, I need to put her to bed." He held out his arms to the baby, but he was utterly astounded when Carlie said suddenly, "No!"

"Her first word is *no*?" Mark blurted, staring at his daughter.

"No!" Carlie repeated.

"I guess she told you," Felipe snickered.

"Six months old and she's already saying no to me? And you need to get our assorted parents and in-laws speaking again," he told Felipe.

"Why me? I'm not responsible for this mess," his brother protested.

"Oh, you're not?"

"Well, maybe indirectly,"

"Try directly. You told Rosemary that you were going to get a justice of the peace to marry you. I heard her screeching it in her room," Mark added. "Maybe she wants a priest."

"She's not catholic. Why couldn't I get Gabriel to do it? You can't get much holier than an angel."

"I don't think he's available. And did you just hear yourself? You said *I*, not *we*. You can't make decisions for Rosemary; you have to involve her. *That's* your problem. Try asking instead of telling," he said, again holding out his arms to the baby.

"No!" Carlie shrieked, repeating it for good measure.

"Carlita, I'm not ready for this." He sighed and sat down beside them. "I guess we're putting on a concert for the princess."

They went through two verses of "Scandal" before Carlie finally fell asleep. As Mark settled her on his shoulder, he told his brother, "I'll put her to bed then deal with Mama and Papa. You're on your own with Lucas and Mary. And good luck with Rosemary." He grinned sarcastically. "Watch out for flying objects."

"Why on earth are Adam and Miss Wings shrieking at each other?" said Mallory, pausing in the doorway.

"Ask Felipe. It has something to do with diamonds."
He put his free arm around her. "And if Carlie says no
to you tomorrow, it's all his fault."

Sighing, Felipe closed the lid on the piano and
trudged reluctantly into the kitchen where his prospec-
tive in-laws were still arguing.

"Do you two love each other?" he asked abruptly,
startling them into silence. Mary gazed at him with
wide green eyes, stunned by the question.

"Why of course we do, Felipe," she said finally, Lucas
nodding in agreement.

"Then why are you arguing about something so
silly?" His arms crossed, he looked at Lucas and added,
"You were just trying to support my father, weren't you?"

Lucas heard the hint in his future son-in-law's
words, and took it, saying quickly, "I thought he needed
a friend. The poor guy looked like he had been kicked
in the gut."

"He did seem pretty miserable," Mary conceded.
Her anger dying, she eyed Lucas warily and asked,
"That was all it was? You weren't trying to pick a fight
with me?"

"God's nightgown, Mary! Why would I do that? I
hate fighting," he said flatly.

"Oh, Lucas, so do I. I'm sorry I snapped at you."

"Honey, believe me, so am I."

Felipe looked at the two of them hugging and
sighed again.

"Well, that was easier than I thought. Something
tells me my parents aren't going to be as agreeable as
you," he said ruefully. "But that is Marcos's problem.

My particular problem is probably using my picture as a dartboard."

"You might want to bring her some flowers," suggested Lucas.

"I don't know, sir. I'd like to get her something that isn't expected, something different," He added wryly, "Something she won't throw at me."

He left the two of them making up in the kitchen and headed back to his piano to think. Candy, flowers, and everything else he could think of were all too predictable.

"Try thinking outside the box," the soft voice said behind him, and Felipe nearly slammed the piano lid on his hand. Apparently Gabriel wasn't done with them yet.

"I'm afraid the box is empty, Gabriel." He flexed his fingers and began playing a piece he had written years before, one that had never made its way onto his brother's playlist. Gabriel swirled his robe around him as he sat down on the bench and listened.

"I like this," he announced finally. "You should record it, Felipe. Call it "Rosemary's Theme." She cannot throw it at you." The archangel reached inside his robe. "Nor can she throw *this*."

He was holding a tiny ball of white fur. It had one blue eye, one green, and it was purring as he handed it to a speechless Felipe.

"It needs a home. I saw that it was abandoned and decided to bring it to you...to give to Rosemary." He rose from the bench and stood gazing at Felipe. "Try to remember that she needs a husband, not a father. She already has Lucas. Now I am leaving, I hope."

"This is a cat," Felipe said stupidly, staring at its pure-white fur.

"I see nothing gets by you. Actually, it's a kitten."

"I don't know if she even likes cats—er—kittens." The poor little thing was so thin he wondered when it had last eaten.

"She does." He glanced upward. "Please tell Adam to stop being a stubborn Irishman and get Carlotta a diamond before she throws things at him—*sharp* things."

"Yes, sir," murmured Felipe as the archangel vanished.

"Well, little guy—or girl—let's see about getting you some food." He cradled the tiny kitten against him as he went back to the kitchen. Lucas and Mary, thankfully, had already vanished up the back stairway. The kitten poked its tiny nose into the milk Felipe poured out and promptly choked.

"I'm not sure what to do with you, little one. I've never had a pet before." He waited until it had lapped up some of the milk and settled the tiny creature in his jacket pocket. "I just hope Rosemary likes you," he muttered as it mewed. Pausing in front of her door, he gave a tentative knock.

"Go away, Felipe! I'm not marrying you!"

"Please open the door, sweetie," he pleaded. "Just let me say one thing to you and then I'll go away." He heard the muffled noises and words—probably cursing at him—and then the door flew open.

"One thing," Rosemary snapped, then gasped as he held the kitten out to her.

"Will you marry *us*?"

⌇

Down the hallway, another heated quarrel was faring much worse, despite Mark's repeated pleas for peace. This was a totally new situation for him; he couldn't remember Adam and Carlotta even raising their voices at each other, let alone throwing things. As a shoe flew past him, he grabbed his tiny mother quickly.

"Mama, you have to stop! Throwing things isn't going to help." As Carlotta erupted into more colorful Spanish, Adam snapped belligerently, "And what kind of nonsense is she saying now?"

"Papa, you don't want to know," Mark said hastily, releasing her. "She doesn't mean it anyway."

"Do not be telling me what I mean, Marcos! I am not a child!"

Deciding to try a new tactic and hoping she wouldn't throw the other shoe at him, Mark yelled back, "Then stop acting like one!"

The words died on her lips as Carlotta stood frozenly, her angry eyes now focused on her son. Had he ever defied her? Had he ever been anything but a model child? And now he was insulting her?

"You dare to—"

"Yes," Mark said quietly. "I dare."

Without a word, Carlotta picked up her other shoe and stalked from the bedroom.

"Well, that went well," the singer said, sighing.

"Laddie, do you think that was wise?" Adam sank down on the loveseat heavily. His shirt was rumpled, he looked exhausted, and there was a small cut on his cheek—most likely from Carlotta.

"You're bleeding," his concerned son said, hurriedly getting a tissue. He sat down beside his father and daubed at the single drop of blood.

"She may be tiny but she doesn't know her own strength," Adam said ruefully.

"I've never seen that side of Mama. Even as a child I can't remember you arguing."

"We did." Adam passed a hand through his greying blond hair. "But we tried to not let you and Felipe see it."

"I suppose I better talk to her." He rose from the loveseat, eying his father's wan complexion worriedly. The normally ruddy skinned Irishman looked on the verge of collapse. "Papa, why don't you go to bed? I'll go look for Mama." He tried to reassure him but Adam was having none of it.

"I must wait up for her, Mark."

"At least rest here." He coaxed Adam to lean back against the cushion and tucked a throw around him. And how many times has he done this for me? Mark wondered, overcome by emotion.

"She's probably outside in the rose garden." He tried to stifle a yawn. "T'is morbid, but she has taken to walking in the cemetery."

The cemetery? It would not be his first choice for a walk. "Do I need body armor, Papa?"

"She would not be hurting you." Adam's tired eyes closed.

"I never thought she would hurt *you*," his son muttered. He was halfway down the hall when Felipe suddenly appeared, a stunned smile on his face.

"Marcos! She said *yes*! We're getting married!" he cried, throwing his arms around his brother.

At least something good was coming out of this night of aggravation and surprises.

"I'm very happy for you, hermanito." He hugged him back, grateful that Felipe seemed to be back to himself at last. "Are you going out to celebrate?"

"Not just yet. I'm going out, but I'm just running to Walmart. We need some things for Snowball," his brother explained.

Why were people talking in riddles today? "Who or what is Snowball?" Mark asked, wondering why Felipe seemed a little nervous.

"Or Marshmallow. We haven't decided yet. Uh, Gabriel gave it to me. I wanted to get Rosemary something unexpected, and he said to give her Snowball. I think that's why she said yes," he said happily.

"Felipe…"

"She's a cat—a kitten, actually. The poor little thing was abandoned," he told his brother. "You don't care, do you, Marcos? We'll take care of her."

So now they had a pet, as well as a resident archangel. Mark sighed and patted his arm. "No, Felipe."

Felipe saw him grabbing his jacket. "You planning on coming with me?"

"No, I'm looking for Mama. She ran off."

Felipe stood stock-still and eyed his brother in amazement. "She *what*?"

"Ran off. She scratched up Papa's face, threw a shoe at him, and is taking a stroll in the rose garden—so he thinks. I'm going to talk to her and drag her back to the house if I can. She may throw the other shoe at me," Mark said ruefully. He stopped on the veranda and looked at Felipe suddenly.

"Can your errand wait a little, Felipe? It might be better if *you* talked to her. She's not too fond of me at the moment."

"Why? What did you do, take Papa's side?"

"In a way. She was taking a tantrum; I called her a child." A trace of bitterness in his voice, Mark added, "Papa didn't deserve what she did."

Felipe leaned against the banister and said flatly, "Marcos, this isn't about a ring; it can't be."

"No," the superstar agreed.

"It's something else."

"I don't know what it could be, Felipe. She's got us, Papa, Carlie, a grandchild on the way—I don't know what could be bothering her."

"Maybe she misses being an angel," Felipe said very quietly.

Disbelief

A homesick angel. Was it possible? Felipe wondered, staring at the motionless figure on the stone bench.

His mind flashed back to a conversation he and Marcos had with Adam, when his father had insisted that, "Carlie is my wife. She goes where I go.'" Had Adam considered Carlotta's feelings? Had he really thought about the consequences to his marriage?

But she had said it was her decision, he remembered.

"You are not disturbing me, Felipe."

The quiet voice came suddenly, shaking him out of his reverie.

"How did you know it was me?" He gave a start when he saw her gaze was fixed on the marble head-stones gleaming in the moonlight. His hands were jammed in his pockets and he was trembling.

She's staring at her own grave.

"Messengers have heightened senses. Apparently, I have retained that ability," Carlotta said, not even looking up when he sat down beside her.

"I used to think you had eyes in the back of your head when I was little."

"It did not keep you from getting into trouble," she said wryly.

No, it had not. He and Marcos had fought constantly. "Mama…"

"You are wondering why I am here? I find it peaceful."

"Actually, I was wondering why you…er…why you flipped out on Papa. I mean, why did you—"

"I know what the expression means, Felipe."

"You took a tantrum," Felipe said frankly.

Carlotta was silent so long he feared she might be contemplating what to throw at *him*.

"It is appropriate, yes? Marcos said I was acting like a child; children take tantrums." She finally turned her head to look at him. "Oddly enough, you and he never took tantrums. You were both old souls."

"Mama…"

"I know I hurt Adam, and for that I am profoundly sorry." She was staring at the graves again and Felipe gave a little shudder, finally blurting, "Why are you staring at your…your…"

"Grave? Does it matter? I am not in it," Carlotta said, shrugging dismissively.

Aha. So he had been right. He said shrewdly, "That's part of the problem, isn't it? You miss being an angel. That's why you flipped out on Papa. You know he wants to stay here and you have doubts. You're just not sure. The ring issue wasn't even important."

His mother gave a very slight nod. "You are partly right. I am not sure how we are going to adjust to this new life. It is very confusing. I am taking my insecurities out on your papa and it is not right." She added ruefully, "You would have made a good priest."

"I'm afraid I like women too much," Felipe murmured. He touched her hand. "So what are you going to do about your problem?"

Sighing, Carlotta rose from the bench. "There is no problem. I am Adam's wife; my place is by his side. I can be happy wherever he is."

"That's crap. You're not happy and you know it." He too rose. "I'm talking to Papa."

An alarmed Carlotta said quickly. "No, you will not. I forbid it, Felipe."

"Mama, in case you haven't noticed, I'm a grown man. I don't need your permission."

"Then he will feel guilty and we both will be unhappy! Is that what you want?" she demanded.

She was right. If he said anything at all to Adam, his canny father would suspect the truth. And nothing would be gained by it.

"Fine. I'll respect your wishes even though I don't agree with you," he said shortly. "But what are you going to say? He's going to want to know what brought this on so suddenly; so would I, for that matter. It can't just have been me fighting with Rosemary."

"Is it important? It is impossible, anyway." She tossed off the words bitterly then broke away from him to run to the house, leaving Felipe to stare after her, baffled.

"What's impossible?" But she ignored him and ran on, straight into Mark, nearly knocking him over.

"Papa's right, you don't know your own strength," her older son said, staggering slightly. And why was she running anyway? Had Felipe said something to upset her?

Carlotta was breathing heavily as she pulled away from him. "I must go to him, Marcos."

"He's sleeping. He's pretty upset, Mama."

She heard the slight reproach in his voice, gave a stifled sob, and ran up the steps.

"What did you say to her?" he asked as Felipe reached him.

"Threatened to tell Papa the truth. Long story short, I'm a bad boy. Your turn, hermano." He pulled his car keys from his jacket pocket. "I'm going to Walmart."

"I'm coming with you." He turned his head to glance at the window of his parents' room. "Let's hope they will have made up by the time we get back."

"Or that Papa finds out what's so impossible," Felipe agreed ruefully.

—

But a guilt-stricken Carlotta had not made it to their bedroom. Instead, she was intercepted by Rosemary. Snowball in her arms, she demanded of her future mother-in-law, "What's going on, Barbie? You two are fighting worse than Felipe and me. And you're angels!"

"We *were* angels. Now we are here."

Rosemary heard the slight catch in her voice and said shrewdly, "And you don't want to be."

"I have already had this conversation with Felipe. I can be happy anywhere that Adam is."

"So why aren't you?"

Tired, dejected, and utterly heartbroken at her behavior with Adam, Carlotta said wearily, "I see I will have to tell you something I did not wish to, or you will keep pestering me, yes? I am not unhappy so much as I am envious." Sighing, she took a deep breath. "You are pregnant. So is Mary." Her hands clenched into fists. "You may make of that what you wish, Rosemary."

Carlotta was across the hall and into her room before her future daughter-in-law could respond. As her husband sighed in his sleep, she dropped down on the floor beside him and reached for his hand.

"Carlie?" Adam was still partially asleep.

"I am so sorry." She touched the cut on his cheek, feeling miserable inside. "Marcos was right; I was acting like a child. I was coveting their pregnancies and I took it out on you." As Adam slowly sat up, Carlotta added humbly, "I will be grateful for what I have. The heavenly father has blessed me with this new chance and I will make the best of it." Her bottom lip wobbled as she said, "And beg your forgiveness for hurting you, Adam."

He lifted her off the floor and onto his lap, hugging her tightly.

"We have baby Carlie, and Felipe and Rosemary will soon bless us with a new grandchild. I was wrong to lash out at you. Wicked," she whispered tearfully.

"No, my love. You are bored," said Adam.

Carlotta eyed her husband as though he had lost his mind.

"I do not understand."

"Think, Carlie. In heaven we were always busy. Even in Loquesta you had the boys to look after. What do you have to do here? What do *I* have to do?"

As his wife pondered his earnest words, she said finally, "I had not considered that, Adam. I will talk to Marcos."

"We are dependent on our sons for everything," said Adam. "And it should not be that way."

It was a sentiment Carlotta later voiced to her elder son.

"Your papa would like a job," she said, and Mark promptly choked on his tea.

"Job?" he managed to squeak. An angel working?

"Are there factories in Los Angeles?"

He had no control over his father; he couldn't tell Adam not to do anything, but this notion of him working was bizarre. Not just because his son was one of the richest men in America, it just wasn't right. Shouldn't Adam be enjoying his retirement?

"Mama…"

"He is bored, Marcos. There is nothing for him to do." As Mark stared at her, Carlotta added, "I am worried about him. He is too restless." Shaking her head at Adam's nocturnal habits, she told her son, "He cannot even sleep; he has taken to walking in the grounds."

And thinking what he might be doing instead, Mark realized, feeling guilty at his oversight. Of course, he was bored, "the emissary from a higher power" had no one to save or even help.

But a job? "I don't think working is the answer, Mama. I think he needs a hobby."

He was to remember her words later; her plaintive confession of Adam's insomnia, and wish that he had paid more attention. So much could have been avoided.

"A hobby?" his mother asked doubtfully. Had Adam ever had one besides singing?

"He's quite proficient at taking things apart." Mark rolled his eyes. "Maybe he could build them."

Adam had already tried taking apart the DVD player, the computer, and the microwave—all to see how they worked. I can't keep up with him, the superstar thought ruefully. Heck, he had even tried to figure out the security system—with disastrous results. The police had shown up, much to Mark's dismay and amusement.

"I'll find something for him to do," he promised Carlotta.

—≈—

But fate, and possibly Gabriel, intervened once more –in the guise of a person Mark had never wanted or expected to see again. He had just concluded a special concert to aid breast cancer and was waiting for Felipe. The Porsche was in for routine maintenance.

"I can take him home," Mallory said to her brother-in-law.

"You sure, Mallie? He might be a little longer."

"Why would I mind? And you and Rosemary are taking Miss Wings and Adam out to dinner, aren't you?"

"Aja! I almost forgot about that," said Felipe. "I'll go tell Marcos that you're his ride."

He had barely gone off to the dressing room when a tall blonde woman seemed to appear. That she was

tanned and beautiful didn't mean anything to Mallory;
it was the very legitimate backstage pass in her hand
that drew her attention.

One of Felipe's former flames? Mallory wondered,
not really caring for the girl's looks at all. *She seems*—
Mallory paused to think of the word—*hard.*

"If you're looking for Felipe…"

The leggy blonde seemed to snicker. "Fat chance of
that, sweetheart. We never did get along. I'm looking
for Mark."

Oh, was she now? "Why?" Mallory asked, not bothering to keep the coolness from her voice.

"I need a reason? If you must know, he and I are old
friends—very intimate friends, if you catch my meaning. Now, would you please be a sweetie and get him?"

"Let's get two things straight." Mallory drew herself
up her full height. "I am not your sweetheart, and I
refuse to let you anywhere near Mark."

"Oh really? What are you, his keeper?" the
blonde sneered.

"She's his wife," Felipe said from behind them, his
voice frosting the words.

The blonde was so startled she dropped the pass.
"Wife?" she blurted, looking stupefied as her eyes slid
from Felipe to Mallory and back again.

"Hello, Hollie," Felipe said curtly.

She was Hollie? The golden girl who had ditched
Mark and inspired "Scandal"?

"Felipe." Hollie said with a disdainful sniff.

"Why are you here?" demanded Felipe, not bothering to hide his coldness.

"Isn't that between Mark and me? It's really none of your business."

"Yes, it is. You left him and I had to pick up the pieces."

"Well, you must have put him back together, or he wouldn't have married Miss Fun Size here." This time, the sniff was directed at Mallory.

Miss Fun Size?

Trying to keep her temper in check, Mallory said sweetly, "Good things come in small packages. And I don't think my husband wants to see you."

"Oh, please, get him, Mallie. He needs to see how lucky he is," said Felipe, scowling.

Still not entirely sure, Mallory gave her brother-in-law a doubtful look as she walked slowly to the gold-starred door.

"No, Papa, you have to press..." Mark broke off as he saw his wife in the doorway. "Never mind. Don't do anything. I'll show you when I get home." Smiling in fond exasperation, he told her, "Papa seems to have messed up the security system again. I'm just glad the police didn't show up this time." He saw the distracted look she wore and asked quickly, "What's wrong, love?"

"Do you think I'm too short?" Mallory blurted, still perturbed by the comment.

"I think you're perfect," her husband answered, puzzled. "Why are you asking?"

"You have a visitor."

"One that said you were short?" Mystified, Mark asked, "Is this someone I don't want to see? Or someone *you* don't want me to see?"

"Both, I hope," she said tersely.

"Aha. This must be a girl—one you don't care for."

"Me? You should see Felipe. He's positively glaring at her."

"I can only think of one girl who affected my brother like…" his words trailed off as sudden realization dawned—and disbelief. Not after all this time. "No. No, she wouldn't dare."

"She dared."

Hollie *here*. The stunned singer leaned against the sofa, his thoughts of the past abruptly crowding into his mind. She had broken up with him so coldly.

It had been another concert, and he had been toying with the idea of breaking things off with her. More and more, he was seeing what Felipe and the others had tried to tell him—that Hollie was not what he wanted her to be; she was a golden girl in disguise. He hadn't wanted to believe them.

But suddenly there was Felipe, a gentleness in his voice as he held his phone out to him.

"Why are you giving me your phone, hermanito? I do have one of my own."

Felipe seemed to be bracing himself. "Yours doesn't have this message on it. It's Hollie. She couldn't tell you herself so she sent it to me." The smile died on Mark's lips as Felipe added gently, "I'm afraid she's breaking up with you. I'm sorry, Marcos." He put an arm around him as his brother took the phone and read words that no girl had ever said to him.

"Why did she break up with you?" Mallory asked curiously.

"The message said she found someone better suited." Mark snickered. "She found a sucker with more money. Matthew has a dot-com empire." He shook his head. "The mere fact that she's here can mean only one thing. Matthew is broke."

"You forgot one. He could have dumped *her*," Mallory suggested.

Sudden surprise and then revengeful satisfaction erased the frown on his face. "I hadn't thought of that. Maybe he did. Maybe he wised up and got bored with having a trophy girlfriend."

"Trophy?"

"He's nearly thirty years older than her," Mark said curtly. "I had him investigated."

A shocked Mallory blurted, "She left you for a man old enough to be her father? Is she insane?"

"Just money hungry. I wasn't rich enough for her."

"Do you want to see her?"

"Not really." Mark pulled on his jacket before adding, "But I am a little curious. I don't know what she could want."

"I do," Mallory snapped. "She wants *you*. And I don't appreciate her calling me Miss Fun Size." As her husband laughed, she added tersely, "It's not funny, Mark."

The singer drew her into his arms. "You're my Miss Fun Size, cara." He tipped up her face. "How does Papa say it? Arun moi chroi," Mark said softly in Gaelic.

Love of my heart. Mallory blinked back tears and brushed a kiss on his lips.

"Go see your gold digger. I'll wait here."

"You aren't going to protect me?"

"You've got Felipe for that."

And his brother was indeed in the protective mode, arms crossed, eyes like chips of blue ice as he glared at the girl who had broken his brother.

But had she? Mark wondered, staring impersonally at Hollie. Once, he had fancied himself in love with her. Once, he had sworn she was the most beautiful woman in the world and he would have done anything for her.

And then he had met Mallory—his Spitfire who had threatened, yelled, slapped, and charmed her way into his life. She had never asked him for anything.

Once, he had been so wrong.

Hollie must have sensed his presence. She turned away from Felipe's glowering figure and smiled at Mark coquettishly.

"Hollie," he said flatly.

"No hug, lover? I came all this way to see you," she pouted.

"Yes, why have you? No cell phones handy?"

"I am so sorry for that." She glanced at Felipe who had planted himself between her and Mark. "Look, can we talk privately—without your shadow?"

"Say what you like. I'd prefer him to stay."

"He might need a witness," Felipe muttered.

"If that's the way you want it."

"Why are you here? Matthew ran out of money? Or did he dump you?"

Something hard entered her eyes. "So you're going to be like that? I hoped we could be civilized, Mark." She scowled. "Fine. You wrote quite a song about me, and you didn't get my permission. 'Scandal' is my song and I want compensation for it."

Never in a million years had Mark expected this, but he should have. She would always be money hungry, always want more.

"Are you insane?" Felipe shouted. "He's not giving you a dime!"

Somewhat recovering his composure, Mark said bluntly, "Explain to me why you think that 'Scandal' is about you."

"Golden girl with heart of stone?"

"I've dated many blondes, Hollie. You weren't the only one that tarnished easily."

"There's no proof 'Scandal' is about you," Felipe hissed, wanting to slap her.

"There's enough to convince a lawyer." Smiling sweetly, she told her former lover, "We could have settled this amiably, Mark. You could have given me a settlement and that would have been the end. Now..." she shrugged.

"Hollie, have you ever heard the expression, veinte la inferno?" As Felipe bit back a snicker, his brother said icily, "In Spanish it means 'go to hell.'" As she gasped, Mark told Felipe, "Have security escort her out."

"You're going to regret this!"

Mark turned around to snap, "The only thing I regret is meeting you."

He was inside his dressing room and didn't hear her scathing reply. A gloating Felipe snatched the pass from the floor and then beckoned to the nearest guard. "Please make sure she leaves—and she's not to be allowed in again."

"Yes, Mr. O'Hara."

"Matthew and I will see you in court," she spat.

"Yeah? You might want to reconsider, sweetheart. You're going to be a laughing stock. What normal woman dumps my brother for an old man?"

Hollie's only response was to give him the finger as the guard led her away.

"I'd like to see you try to sue," Felipe muttered, glaring after her.

In his dressing room, Mark was still shaking with anger. For the first time in his life, he wanted to slap a woman; he wanted to mar her artificial beauty.

"Honey?" Mallory watched in alarm as he balled a fist and punched his traveling bag.

Mark abruptly pulled her into his arms and held her tightly. She tried to pull back to see his face but he said tersely, "Don't let go. I need to hold you. I need to know there's still goodness and real beauty in this world"—he let out a tiny snicker—"Besides, I might hit the lamp next."

Mallory waited until his shaking eased and asked, "What did she want? You?"

Mark finally drew back to gaze at her, his expression scornful. "Oh, no. That I could have handled. No, she wants my royalties from 'Scandal.'"

"What? But they're yours. Why would she think—"

"That she's entitled to them? In a way, she is. I did write the song about her. It was the way she did it— cold, calculating, no morals whatsoever—how could I have been so wrong about her? People tried to tell me; I just wouldn't listen."

"How did you finally—"

"Come to my senses? Oh, that was Felipe. As you can see, he can't stand her."

There was a light tap on the door. Felipe came in and nodded.

"I was trying to explain your part in the Hollie fiasco, Felipe. Do you want to tell Mallory?"

"Oh." He perched on the sofa arm. "She kept breaking dates with him. I got curious." His blue eyes flickered over his brother. "Marcos thought it was something he did—I knew better. So I had her followed and found out she was meeting Matthew."

"Fool that I was, I didn't believe him," Mark said simply.

"So I provided him with proof. Pictures."

"I had to believe him then." Mark's hazel eyes filled with remembered pain. "That hurt. I do have some vanity. I couldn't understand why she was rejecting me for *him*."

"I do. She's a mercenary bitch," Felipe snapped. Turning to Mallory, he added, "He finally wised up. He was going to break off the relationship that day but she beat him to it." His lip curled in contempt. "She sent *me* a message. Coward that she is, she wanted me to tell Marcos she couldn't see him anymore."

"And you haven't had any contact with her since?"

"Not until today." Picking up his traveling bag from the floor, Mark paused and suddenly glanced at Felipe. "This isn't going to be the end of it, is it? She must have known I wouldn't hand over that kind of money. She has plans," Mark said flatly as Felipe nodded.

"I'm afraid so, hermano. We haven't seen the last of her."

Revenge

A fuming, vengeful Hollie stalked through the doors at Infinity, thoughts of her former boyfriend not at all kind. Why, he had sworn at her. She hated the superstar, hated the cool, mocking words and the arrogant way he had behaved.

"So I dumped you," Hollie muttered, plopping herself on the nearest stool. "Big freaking deal. Get over it already."

She ordered white wine and tried to compose herself. Dammit, Mark owed her that money. "Scandal" was a monster hit—all thanks to her.

"Freaking bastard. It's *my* song," she fumed, never even noticing who was sitting beside her.

"Who are you mad at, doll?"

Hollie cast a contemptuous glance at the thin, hawk-nosed man sprawled in the stool on her left.

"Not that it's any of your business but he's a musician. I'm sure you don't know him." She picked up her glass and drained it swiftly, hoping this bar bum would leave her alone.

"Try me." He signaled the waitress. "I used to be a roadie for Mr. Legend himself."

Hollie almost dropped the glass. Swiveling on the stool, she eyed him incredulously. "You have got to be kidding me!"

"Till he fired me"—Mendoza took a sip of his beer—"and blackballed me."

She caught the sneer in his voice.

"So you're pissed at him too?"

"You might say that." He eyed her coolly. She certainly hadn't been with the superstar when he had worked; they must have broken up before the Scandal Tour began. "What's he done to you?"

"Aside from telling me to go to hell? The bastard won't give me the money he owes me."

"For what?"

Now that she had an appreciative audience, Hollie was warming to her subject. "He wrote a song about me—'Scandal.' Have you heard it?"

"Who hasn't?"

"It's my song! *Mine*. And I want paid for it."

Mendoza regarded her thoughtfully, gauging her possible usefulness to him. That she was a gold digger was definitely in her favor—she would likely do anything for money.

"What's your name, doll?"

"Hollie. You don't need to know the rest."

"And you don't need to know mine," he said just as curtly. "What if I could help you get your money, Hollie?"

"Why should you?"

"Because I have a score to settle with Mr. O'Hara. He owes me too—far more than you. Call it *blood* money." When she remained silent, he added, "You don't want to know why?"

"No. I really don't care about other people," she said bluntly.

"Neither do I, doll. Scruples get in the way." He set down his drink and swiveled on his stool to gaze at her. "We got a deal?"

"How do I know you won't keep the money?" she said, suddenly suspicious of his motives.

"I told you. I'm out for blood. You can have the money. Well?"

She stared back at him coolly. She didn't like him, and she still didn't trust him, but if this odd man could get her the money and hurt Mark in the process, why should it matter?

"Deal."

Heartbreak

Mendoza eyed the sleeping baby and wondered how he had been so fortunate. First the gate to the estate had been disarmed—wide open, actually—and the front door had, to his surprise, been unlocked as well. He would have suspected a trap if the whole house hadn't seemed to be asleep.

Like this baby. He knew Mark had a child, but that was the extent of his knowledge. He hadn't planned on taking the infant, but suddenly it seemed like it was the perfect revenge. It was fitting, Mendoza decided, scooping up the child. Blood for blood.

Holding the baby against him and praying it would stay asleep, he crept down the stairs and back out the door. At the bottom of the drive, Hollie was waiting. He was halfway down when he heard the shout behind him.

"Stop!" Adam yelled, recognizing the bastard who had shot at his son. And he had Carlie!

"Sorry, old man!" Mendoza flung the words at him sneeringly.

Adam was running down the drive as fast as he could.

"I want 10 million! Tell him to bring it to Loquesta."

"Saints preserve us!" He couldn't run anymore and leaned against a tree to catch his breath. Up ahead, Mendoza, clutching Carlie like a football, flung more words back at him.

"Too bad, old man!"

"Old?" the former messenger echoed indignantly. Why, he certainly was not an old man. He was in his prime.

But he was 51 years old and feeling every one of them. His knees ached, he was winded, and there was a stitch in his side—problems that would have been unthinkable if he was still an angel. Being a mortal again took some getting used to.

He was old and tired and feeling like he was doing nothing worth his time; nothing productive or useful. "I couldn't even catch the perverted creature," Adam muttered. He saw Mendoza get into a waiting car and his hands balled into fists.

"Sure, and wouldn't I be catching you if I was 20 years younger." Sighing, he trudged back up the driveway, wondering how he was to tell Mark that his baby daughter had been kidnapped and that it was all his fault.

"Stupid and careless," he muttered.

"Naive." The word seemed to leap into his ear, a habit of old.

So the archangel had seen everything. "You are not helping, Gabriel."

He suddenly appeared beside him.

"And you should have listened. Mark tried to explain the security system to you, Adam."

"Aye. That he did." Looking unbearably sad, he added, "Why did this happen?"

"There are reasons."

"She has her guardian?"

"Of course." Gabriel laid a hand on the former messenger's shoulder. "Carlie is in no real danger, Adam. I tell you this because you're reacting as a mortal."

Somewhat stung by the implied criticism, Adam snapped, "The wee lass is my granddaughter!"

"Yes, and as an angel you would realize that certain events have to be set in motion for a final outcome to occur."

"I know that," said Adam.

"But you have obviously forgotten."

"There is nothing more you can tell me?"

"You know I cannot." The archangel's voice was gentle with regret. His hand moved to Adam's cheek. "Go now. You need to tell Mark who took Carlie."

"What is that?" Hollie shrieked.

Mendoza stared at her. "What do you mean, what is it? It's a baby. Mr. O'Hara's baby," he said, smirking. "I took it."

"Mark's baby? Why?"

"You want your money, doll? This brat is our salvation. Mr. O'Hara will pay anything to get it back." He pulled off the road and checked the diaper the baby wore. "It's a girl."

Carlie, puzzled and scared of the strange person who held her, began to wail.

"What are we supposed to do with her?"

"Not we, doll. *You.* Go in that convenience store with her and get some milk. I guess you need diapers, too. Do they eat food?"

"How the hell do I know? I've never been around babies. I don't like babies," Hollie sniffed, taking Carlie gingerly.

"Well, until we get the money, you better take good care of this one. Now hurry up. I think old man O'Hara recognized me."

Sighing, Hollie shifted Carlie against her and hurried into the store.

Diapers…why were there so many?

"Do you talk, baby? I don't know what size to get!"

"Ga?" said Carlie, her blue-green eyes focused on this stranger.

Hollie grabbed a package at random and sped off to get some milk and a bottle. It was when she got to the checkout that she noticed the woman in line staring at her.

"Beautiful baby," said the somewhat pudgy, brown-haired woman, smiling at Carlie. "Boy or girl?"

"Uh…girl," Hollie said hurriedly, remembering Mendoza's words. She grabbed the change and package as the woman asked casually, "What's her name?"

Hollie didn't bother trying to think of a name; she shifted the unhappy Carlie in her arms and ran out of the store.

"That's not her baby," Hannah Carson said grimly.

It was the scream that tore at his heart. Mark stared at the empty crib and wondered if this wasn't a bad dream. Carlie should be sleeping in her crib. Carlie couldn't be kidnapped.

He could almost think it was a nightmare if it wasn't for Mallory screaming.

"She can't be *gone*, Mallory. Maybe my mother or Rosemary has her."

Emerald fire flashed in her eyes as Mallory whirled on him. "Do you think I didn't check, Mark? No one has her! What part of *gone* don't you understand?"

"But the security..." Hadn't Felipe told him it rivaled Fort Knox?

"It's not on." Felipe ran up the steps to them. "The front door is wide open, Marcos."

"What?" Stunned, Mark sank down on the top step and stared open-mouthed at his brother. This couldn't be happening. Not his baby...

He had caused this. His fame had affected an innocent child. He hadn't been able to protect her.

"Snap out of it, Marcos. Someone's taken her and we're going to have to search the grounds. When did you see her last, Mallie?"

Gratified that someone was taking charge, Mallory tried to pull herself together. "It...it was after ten, I think." A sob shook her voice and her hand trailed over the blanket still in the crib. "I fed her." She looked worriedly at her strangely silent husband. Mark seemed to be in a daze. "We were thrilled that she was finally sleeping through the night. She...she was gone, wasn't she?"

"It would seem so, sweetie." Felipe touched her shoulder gently.

From behind them, Carlotta said worriedly, "Your Papa is gone too, Felipe. He has not come back from his walk."

"Maybe he has Carlie," Mallory said hopefully.

"Adam would not do such a thing." She, too, was gazing at her elder son in concern. Marcos seemed frozen.

A dumbfounded Felipe asked, "Papa takes walks in the middle of the night?"

"He cannot sleep," his mother said simply.

The words were scarcely out of her mouth when Adam staggered up the steps. He was dirty, disheveled, and breathing heavily as he held the railing for support. Carlotta sped down to him, putting an arm around him as he told them, "It seems I can't run either." His blue eyes focused on Mark, still slumped on the floor. He was shaking uncontrollably as his father dropped down beside him.

"I don't know what's wrong with Marcos," said Felipe.

"I do." Putting both arms around him, Adam held his son protectively as he told the others, "He thinks it's his fault when it's actually mine. I unlocked the gate. The buttons confused me." Shaking his head, the guilt-stricken grandfather added, "I saw him run off with our Carlie. I tried to stop him but he ran too fast. He called me an old man, and he was right."

"Who, Papa?" asked Felipe.

"The perverted creature who tried to kill your brother at the concert. He did this," hissed Adam.

Like one coming out of a trance, Mark blinked fuzzily at his father. Had he really said…

"Mendoza?" he said faintly. "But he's in prison."

"I saw him, laddie," Adam insisted.

"They wouldn't have released him this soon. He probably escaped," muttered Felipe. He watched as his brother seemed to wrench himself back to a grim reality. "One, two, three…"

"That bastard took my daughter?" the superstar shouted.

"There we go," said Felipe and Adam nodded.

"Mendoza!" shrieked Mallory and Rosemary simultaneously.

"Aye. Best get out your pocket telephone, Mark. He'll be calling about a ransom."

"But he doesn't know my number, Papa."

"Apparently he knows mine"—Felipe stared at his phone—"which doesn't make sense since I never gave it to him."

"Aren't you going to talk to him, laddie?"

"It's a message, Papa." Felipe stared at the tiny screen, a look of utter astonishment on his face.

"Felipe," Mark said impatiently, holding out his hand.

His brother gave him the phone. 'Be at Allied tonight at seven. Bring 10 million. You call the cops and your brat gets it.'

"Allied?" Adam echoed, mystified. "*My* Allied?"

"He's talking about the old factory in Loquesta? But the whole town was supposedly bulldozed! It's a landfill now. That doesn't…wait a minute." Felipe's incredulous gaze slid from Adam to Mark. "How does *he* know about Allied? And why would he take Lovey all that way, Marcos?"

"The faugh mentioned Loquesta. And he said it with an accent, laddie."

"There is something fishy going on, Marcos," Carlotta announced.

The wheels were finally turning in Mark's mind, and he came to a startling conclusion.

"No, Mama." He gave a rueful snicker. "I should have figured it out before when he went there and found Papa. Who in their right mind goes to that hellhole? Who's even heard of it?"

"But Gabriel and I arranged that, Mark," said Adam.

"You didn't have to in Mendoza's case. Don't you understand? He's from Loquesta."

Malice

Carlie had flown many times in her short life, but always in the Santa Belle with her father as pilot. Never in a rattletrap plane that looked like it was held together with duct tape.

Her blue-green eyes fastened on the loud man who was arguing with the strange woman who held her so gingerly.

"You really expect to fly to Santa Fe in this thing?" Hollie asked dubiously. "Do you know how far that is, genius?"

"I know exactly how far it is," Mendoza retorted.

"Why are we going there, anyway? You couldn't have met him in LA?" she demanded, shoving a bottle at Carlie.

"Mr. O'Hara and I have a history. Let's just say I want him to be reminded of it."

"Well, I'll be glad when it's over. This baby gives me the willies."

"Why? She doesn't even cry."

"She's just strange. It's her eyes. It's like she can see right through you." Hollie shuddered. "And she keeps saying ga."

"Ga," echoed Carlie, stretching out her hand.

"See?"

In another part of LAX, a very somber group boarded
the Santa Belle. Adam had slipped into the copilot's
seat beside his silent son. Carlotta was sitting quietly
beside Steve. Rosemary was eyeing her morose twin
as she slumped in her seat, her hand clutching one of
Carlie's stuffed animals. Felipe's protective gaze slid
back and forth between his pregnant fiancée and his
brother. Mark hadn't said one word since he had started
the small jet's engine, just the terse "roger, tower," as it
roared down the runway. Adam busied himself check-
ing various gauges. From time to time he would glance
at his son, an action that seemed to irritate the singer.

"Don't."

"Laddie?"

"Don't look at me like that. You're feeling sorry
for me."

"No, Mark. I am wondering how you're coping. I
couldn't," Adam said simply.

"Yes, you could, Papa—you're the strongest man I
know." His voice suddenly trembled. "I'm trying to be
strong, but I can't help thinking that he…he hates me,
Papa!"

"Laddie, he's not going to hurt the wee lass. He
wants money."

"Is your crystal ball telling you that?" the singer
muttered, abruptly wishing that his father was still a
messenger. He could save her.

But he hadn't reckoned on the voice in his ear.

How do you know he won't? He is her grandfather.

"Yes, he is," Mark bowed his head, feeling ashamed.

"Let's just say I've seen his kind before." The older man shook his blond head in disgust. "'Tis lacking in morals they are."

Despite the grief and anger preying heavily on his mind, Mark asked curiously, "You mean in heaven?"

"Heaven *and* earth."

They had never discussed his angelic experiences. Would he tell him anything? Was he even allowed? "Did...did you help a lot of people, Papa?"

"I'd like to think so. T'was hard sometimes, not knowing if you were getting through," said Adam ruefully.

"You must have. Gabriel said Felipe was one of your few failures." The words were out of his mouth before he realized how it would affect his father. To his shame, Mark saw tears brighten Adam's blue eyes.

"Papa, I'm sorry. I shouldn't have..."

"Why? Gabriel was right." Pain choking his words, he muttered, "Aye, I should have seen it. What kind of angel am I—was I—not to see why my own child was suffering?"

Neither of them was aware that Felipe was listening until he said haltingly, "Maybe I had to go through it just to realize what an ass I was. And you didn't fail, Papa. You and Mama stopped me from swallowing the pills, twice. So you did save my life," Felipe said earnestly, putting a hand on Adam's shoulder.

Overcome with emotion, Adam choked out, "Thank you, Felipe."

But he couldn't save Carlie, Mark realized bitter-sweetly. There was only one angel that could, and he doubted Gabriel would get involved. Rules mustn't be broken.

The next moment, the Santa Belle nearly went into a nosedive as Mark heard Gabriel murmur, "Your daughter has her own guardian angel, Mark."

"Saints preserve us!" cried his father, swiftly taking the controls. "Mark, what's gotten into you?"

As the others looked on in shock and disbelief, Mark demanded of Adam, "Is it true, Papa? Carlie has a guardian angel?"

Adam set the small jet back on course before telling his son, "Of course she does. Everyone has one. Even that perverted Mendoza, though he chooses not to listen." He hesitated, mindful of Steve's presence in the cabin, "Gabriel spoke to you?"

"Your friend has a bad sense of timing." There was a very tiny smile on his lips. "Felipe's probably up to four Our Fathers by now."

"Five," said Felipe, getting off the floor.

"You wanna watch it, honey? I'm pregnant, remember?" said Rosemary.

"Carlie?" Adam glanced back over his shoulder anxiously.

"I am fine, Adam. But please warn us, Marcos, next time you intend to do a dipsy," Carlotta told her elder son sternly.

"Sorry, everyone." Under his breath, Mark muttered, "It's all Gabriel's fault."

The words seemed to leap into his ear. "But I am not flying the plane, Mark."

Mallory saw the brief exasperation flit across his face as he touched a hand to his ear and knew the archangel was communicating with her husband. "It's Gabriel, isn't it? You're talking to him." She grabbed at Mark's shoulder, her grief making her hysterical, "He knows about my baby, he knows if she's okay—"

"Mallory," Mark began, feeling helpless.

"Mallie?" Steve asked worriedly. If they didn't find Carlie soon, he feared for her sanity.

"I need to know if she's alive!" cried Mallory, her fist pounding Mark's arm.

"I can handle the landing, laddie," Adam told his troubled son.

Mark nodded and swiftly urged his now-weeping wife into the cabin.

"We can't tell Steve about Gabriel, love."

"Do you think I care, Mark? I want Carlie!"

"He says she has her own angel." Mark tried to comfort her but she was having none of it.

"Oh, really? Well, it didn't stop her from getting kidnapped!" She pushed his arms away.

Mark squeezed his eyes shut and plaintively whispered the archangel's name. There was a great rustle of wings as Gabriel suddenly appeared before them.

"You do realize that others need me, Mark? And why would you let Adam land the plane?"

"He has before."

"He was a messenger then."

"He's forgotten more than I'll ever learn. And I've trusted him with my life before." As the plane slowly began its descent, Mark added, "He's landing now."

"Where's Carlie?" Mallory begged Gabriel.

"I can only tell you she's fine. She's not in any real danger."

"Then why can't you bring her to us?"

"You know I cannot get involved." He reached out and put his hands on her shoulders. "I told you this world takes courage, Mallory, remember?"

"You were talking about *Carlie*?"

A great sadness filled his face. "No," he said simply. His wings shimmered and he was gone.

"Wait, what? What's he talking about?"

"Cara, you need to sit down. Papa's landing." Mark tried to guide her to the nearest seat but she brushed off his hand again.

"Why is he saying I need courage?"

"I don't know, love. But we're in Santa Fe now. I'm sure we'll find out. Papa and I have to meet him in two hours."

~~

One of those hours had already passed when Mallory suddenly burst into the living room of the penthouse and grabbed her husband's arm. "He was talking about you!" she cried as the others looked on in silent sympathy. "He didn't mean Carlie at all. Mendoza is going to kill you! He's just using Carlie as bait!"

She was verging on hysteria. Mark looked over at Steve and nodded, then swiftly picked up his weeping wife in his arms, carrying her into the master bedroom of the suite.

"He's going to kill you," she sobbed.

Summoning up a smile, Mark said gently, "He's not that smart, cara. I'm a streetfighter, remember?"

"You aren't even armed—"

"I can't risk Carlie's life, Mallory."

"I want my baby…"

"And I will bring her back to you." He sat on the bed, cuddling her against him as Steve swiftly gave her a shot.

"You're a ghoul, Steve," Mallory whispered tearfully.

"I know, honey. You rest now." He glanced at Mark in sympathy as the distraught superstar covered his wife with a throw, kissed her, and hurriedly left the room.

"Let's get this over with, Papa." He was almost to the door when he stopped abruptly and went to where Rosemary was huddled with Felipe.

"If something happens to me…"

"Marcos." Felipe reached out and grabbed his hand briefly.

"Look after her." As Rosemary gave a tearful nod, Mark pressed his brother's hand in return and smiled reassuringly at Carlotta. He followed Adam from the suite and hurriedly left the hotel.

They had just left the parking lot when Adam said suddenly, "I'm remembering another trip we took on this road."

That day, that trip had been a happy occasion. Adam and his grungy, black overcoat and the secret he had been hiding. Once a dedicated messenger, now a doting grandfather. It had been so simple then.

Now he had to jump through hoops—and what if he didn't make it?

"Papa, you have to promise me something."

One look at the stubbornness on his son's face and Adam said flatly, "No, Mark, I will not. I will not even consider it."

"You don't know—"

"Yes, laddie, I do," Adam interrupted. "You're wanting me to look after the assorted members of our family, and I will not do it."

"Why?" Mark burst out. "Papa, you do realize that Mendoza could kill me?"

"Aye. I also realize he's a lousy shot."

They were almost to what was left of Loquesta. He could see the burnt-out shell of the factory. Mark glanced over at Adam, wondering how the former angel would deal with the scene of his death.

"'Tis just a building, laddie."

"A building that killed you."

Suddenly, he saw Adam put a hand to his ear.

"Papa?"

"The will of God will never take you where the grace of God will not protect you." The older man sighed. "It's one of Gabriel's favorite expressions. And that I look like crap."

"Quite a sense of humor he has." They were circling the remains of the plant. Felipe had gotten another message, telling him Mendoza would be in the back by the old loading dock. Just another clue that he was from the blighted town.

"I've never been here." There was debris everywhere, leaving no more room to drive. He saw an old vehicle, presumably Mendoza's, parked to the side. "I guess we're walking from here, Papa."

"'Tis a walk I'm very familiar with, Mark."

They turned the corner and he could see his former roadie up ahead. Mendoza was clutching Carlie like a football, paying no attention to her whatsoever. Mark felt a murderous rage bubble up inside him, wishing he could kill him. Here, on these streets of injustice and squalor, the blood lust returned with a vengeance. He wanted Mendoza to be his last victim.

"You still sensing my thoughts, Papa?" He shifted the bag with the money to his other arm.

"Aye. The good Lord will take care of him, Mark," Adam said, scowling at the ex roadie.

"What is that behind him?" The ground seemed to fall away, like the edge of a ravine.

"'Tis where we used to dump the defects. Just a garbage pit."

They were less than ten feet away. Mendoza, a sneer in his voice, snapped, "Stop right there. You come any closer and this brat gets it." He was holding a gun in his other hand—a gun which was aimed at Carlie's red curls. The sight terrorized Mark. He fought back the pain and bile bubbling up inside and said, "I'm not armed and neither is my father. They money's all there. Just give me my daughter—please!"

"Gee, you're begging. I like that." His gray eyes bore into Mark. "You don't know who I am, do you? Or why I hate your guts?"

"I know you're from here. That's how you were able to add information to my wife's article," Mark said, fighting the panic that was holding him frozen.

"Yeah, I was raised in this dump. I knew you. But you knew my brother far better. You killed him, you son of a bitch. His name was Antonio," Mendoza hissed as Mark's jaw dropped. As the truth imploded in his mind, the former roadie said scathingly, "Remember him, you murderer?"

How could he forget the crumpled body on the ground? Tonio had cut him, threatened Felipe, and vowed to bring down a far superior street fighter. But as the unbidden memory washed over Mark, he remembered something that had puzzled him. He had sworn that he killed Tonio; after all, he wasn't moving, but there was not that much blood. Not nearly enough for a fatal wound.

"He was going to cut a 13-year-old boy!" Mark cried in protest.

"I don't care," Mendoza shrugged. "You killed the only person that ever mattered to me." He motioned to the satchel. "Kick the bag over here."

When Adam had done so, Mendoza smirked and said, "So you're not armed?"

"I told you I wasn't. I don't lie."

"Too bad. Here's your brat." He flung Carlie toward her father as he added contemptuously, "The money's not for me, but this is for you...for Antonio."

As the bullet whizzed toward Mark, things seemed to happen simultaneously. He felt Adam shove him out of the way as Gabriel, his enormous wings fluttering, swooped down and grabbed the terrified Carlie.

"What the hell!" Mendoza screamed and began edging backward, not realizing the garbage dump was behind him. With another terrified cry, he went over the edge.

"Not quite," said Gabriel, trying to soothe the baby.

"Saints preserve us—the bastard shot me!" Adam cried, staring at the blood staining his shirt.

"Papa?" Mark cried in alarm.

"He's okay. It just grazed his shoulder." Gabriel handed Carlie to her father and shook his head at the former messenger. "The bullet was meant for you, Mark. You knew that and you faced him anyway."

"I had to save Carlie. I didn't care what happened to me."

"Am I dying?" Adam asked haltingly, still eying the blood.

"Oh, good grief." Gabriel pressed his hand to the wound. "Adam, you continue to interfere, even as a mortal. It's a flesh wound! We're not ready for you to come back yet."

"Dada," said Carlie, patting his cheek.

Tears were running down Mark's face. She was dirty and her diaper needed changing, but she was *alive*.

"Is the wee lass okay?" Adam asked anxiously.

"I would say she needs a bath." Gabriel picked up the satchel and set it by Mark.

"Is he—"

"Dead? Yes," the archangel said soberly. "He fell on a pile of old, rusted machinery." He glanced at the ravine. "Loquesta *has* claimed its last victim."

"Gabriel, I'm thinking I may need stitches."

"No, you need a Band-Aid," Gabriel retorted. Exasperated, he told Mark, "Please, look after him." He touched Mark's cheek briefly then dropped his hand to Carlie's red curls. There was a great rustle of gossamer wings as he disappeared from their view.

"This was all because I tried to protect Felipe?" Mark said in disbelief.

Adam, finally convinced his wound wasn't fatal, said abruptly, "No, Mark, that's not quite how it happened. Let's go back to the hotel and I'll explain."

Mallory sobbed in her sleep. It was a bad dream—a nightmare, actually—that had Mendoza laughing demonically and tormenting Mark. He seemed to be throwing something.

But at who? And why couldn't she see what it was?

In the living room of the penthouse, Steve was telling a relieved Mark, "I don't see any signs of injury. She's cranky, dirty, and probably hungry. Give her a bath then feed her, amigo."

"No!" said Carlie.

"I guess she told you, Steve," her father chuckled.

"Mama," was the baby's response.

"Lovey, you learned a new word," Felipe said, smiling at his niece.

"She sure did. And I think I better take her to Mallory, dirty or not."

━━

She could almost hear Carlie, and she was calling her Mama. But Mendoza had her, Mallory thought, confused. He wanted his 10 million and he would give her back. But was there really any guarantee that he would? He had raped Rosemary, tried to kill Mark, and kidnapped Carlie—all because he hated the singer. There was no reason he would keep his word. He could keep the money, kill Carlie, and be on his way. And even if he didn't kill her, he could always molest her.

"Kill him," Mallory cried, still in her nightmare world. She felt the hand on her shoulder and struggled up through the layers of drugged oblivion to hear Mark say quietly, "He's already dead, love, thanks to Gabriel."

"Mark?" Her eyes flew open in joy and shock as Carlie suddenly said, "Mama," and reached both arms to her weeping mother.

"Oh, god, my baby! You said you would bring her back to me—thank you!" She grabbed the little girl and pressed her face against Carlie's.

"Gabriel saved her, love. He caught her when Mendoza—"

"He threw her! I saw it in my nightmare," Malloy blurted, clutching Carlie tightly.

"Yes. And then he fired at me. Papa shoved me out of the way and the bullet hit his arm. He's okay, cara," Mark answered hastily, seeing the horror on her pale face.

"He saved you again," Mallory said softly.

"Yes," Mark said, bowing his head.

"I don't understand, Mark, why Mendoza would do this. I know it was revenge, but just because you fired him and then beat him up? There's got to be more to it."

"There is, love. Bring the princess in the living room. Papa has a story to tell us."

Vindication

Carlotta, Felipe, Rosemary, Steve, and Adam were already sitting down when Mark, Mallory, and Carlie came into the living room.

"This is probably the only time I'll ever discuss this." Mark's eyes traveled to Steve. "What I'm about to tell you may be a little hard to understand, but you didn't grow up the same way I did."

"Try me, amigo."

"What could this possibly have to do with Loquesta, Marcos?"

"Everything, Mama. It's why it happened. It started there." He sighed as he turned to Felipe. "This goes back to when Tonio called you a half breed and threatened to cut you, remember?"

"It's a little hard to forget, Marcos. He held a shiv to my throat." Both Carlotta and Rosemary gasped and Felipe said ruefully, "Believe me, it's not something I want to remember. But I don't see—"

"What it has to do with anything?" Mark finished his brother's sentence. "A lot. Tonio's last name was Mendoza. Jerry was his brother."

As his quiet words revealed the truth, the singer added, "Something I never knew until today."

"You killed him to avenge your brother."

"Yes," Mark bowed his head to acknowledge his mother's words.

Steve, his eyes huge, asked in disbelief, "You actually *killed* someone?"

The former street fighter said, "I told you it would be hard to understand." Remembering the gory scene, Tonio in a heap, his body against a trash can, Mark snapped, "It was either him or Felipe." Glancing at Adam, he added, "I'm not proud of what I did but I wasn't raised to turn the other cheek."

"Wait a minute," said Rosemary, leaning forward. "You mean that was the reason? He did all this because you took out his brother?" she demanded incredulously.

"That's what I thought, but according to Papa that's not quite how it happened."

"No, laddie. It was not. You wounded him." Adam's sure words surprised them all. Steve looked bewildered, and Mark and Felipe eyed their father in total astonishment.

'I'm never far from either of my sons.' The former angel's comforting words echoed through Mark's confused mind. He had seen everything. He had seen *what*?

"Papa?"

"You didn't kill him, Mark." Adam sighed and looked over at Steve. "Dr. Steve, would you mind excusing us?"

"Of course, Adam."

Mark waited until his young physician headed into the kitchen before saying, "Would you mind explaining what you mean by that? I know I killed him, Papa. He wasn't moving." Was that why there hadn't been that much blood?

"You wounded him," Adam said again.

"How do you know that?" Mark blurted. "I know I heard you at times—"

"So did I," Felipe interrupted, his statement not really surprising his brother.

"Because I was there. I didn't let you hear me that time, but I was there. I saw everything."

"But I cut him, Papa!"

"Yes, you did," Adam said gravely. "But it was one of his so-called pals who finished him. T'was over money, I'm remembering." Adam shrugged. "He saw you run off and naturally assumed you would be blamed, Mark."

His son looked sick. "All these years I thought I'd killed him—and it was someone *else*?"

As Adam nodded, Mark abruptly remembered something. "You yelled at me, Papa." He shook a finger at his father. "You accused me of playing God and said you were ashamed of me."

"Adam," said Carlotta in reproach.

"I had to, my love. He was determined to go after that faugh. T'was the only way I could stop him." Adam turned back to grin sheepishly at Mark. "Will you be forgiving me, laddie?"

"I don't know." Mark gazed at him in exasperation. "Was it really necessary to give me all those chills and fevers? I thought I was in menopause."

Mallory broke into giggles, a sound that delighted Mark. He'd been half afraid he would never hear her laugh again. Or to see his precious daughter. He watched as Mallory set the little girl on the floor and Carlie suddenly began to crawl across the floor.

"Good lord," said her surprised father.

"It's called crawling, sweetie," said a giggling Rosemary, holding out her arms to her niece. She picked up Carlie, her eyes suddenly focusing on the baby's diaper. "Mallie, would you say most guys know how to change a diaper?"

"Probably not," said her puzzled twin.

"I think I put it on backward the first time I changed her," Mark said, smiling.

"Bingo," Rosemary said softly. "This one is on right. It's too big but it's not on backward."

"What are you getting at, lassie?" Adam asked his future daughter-in-law.

"Mendoza didn't do this. He had help. Probably a woman." Rosemary shrugged.

But the bastard had only just escaped from prison. "Who?" Mark asked blankly. "Who in their right— wait a minute." He snapped his fingers. "He said the money was for someone else. But *who*?"

As it turned out, he didn't have long to find out.

They were back in Los Angeles that night. The next morning, Felipe was startled by a knock at the front door. One of the band that early? "The guys don't usually get up this early," he told Rosemary. Very few people knew the security code.

But it was Hannah Carson who stood in the doorway.

"Hey, it's my fake fiancée," he said with a playful grin.

She didn't return his smile. In fact, the actress looked troubled.

"Hey, Felipe, Rosemary. Can I come in? I need to speak to you."

A puzzled Felipe motioned her inside.

"You're going to think this is a very odd question, but is your niece here?"

Rosemary and Felipe exchanged glances. "Why are you asking, Hannah?"

"Because I saw her. I stopped at a convenience store for coffee and she was there—with a blonde woman," Hannah told them. "I stopped yesterday but no one was here."

"We were in Santa Fe," said Rosemary.

From behind them, Mark said suddenly, "Blonde?"

Hannah nodded at him. "A natural blonde. Tall, leggy, very pretty. She had a butterfly tattoo on her cheek," the Broadway actress said, wondering why the superstar's mouth fell open. He seemed shocked at her words.

Shocked and furious. "Hollie?" Mark hissed. The only woman he knew who had a tattoo on her cheek. The woman who would do anything for money, even kidnap a baby.

"She didn't know the baby's name when I asked her. She just ran out the door."

Hollie kept staring at the door of the ramshackle motel room. Genius hadn't come back from Loquesta and she didn't know what to do. It had been well over two hours since he had left; surely he should have returned by now. Any second now he would walk in with her money—all ten million of it.

But what if he didn't? What if it had gone wrong?

Mark could have outsmarted him. Genius could have talked, could have even revealed her involvement in the baby's kidnapping.

I could go to prison, Hollie thought, shuddering with fright.

Even if Genius didn't know her last name, Mark did.

"That's it! I'm not staying here another minute." She grabbed her purse and ran out the door. At the lobby, she managed to get the dirty man behind the counter to call her a cab.

At the airport, she made a swift call to Matthew. She told her bewildered lover that she would be staying with her cousin and that he wasn't to give any information to anyone about her whereabouts.

She told her cousin the same thing. But she realized, belatedly, that Mark could easily ferret out the information from either of them.

"I am not going to prison," she muttered, eying the gun her cousin kept for protection. She would keep it handy.

Mark would never give her the money now, but maybe he could be persuaded.

The private investigator he had hired had given Mark Matthew's number, and he clicked the numbers angrily, trying to compose himself. He wasn't mad at Matthew.

When the older man finally answered, the singer took a deep breath and said calmly,

"Matthew, this is Mark O'Hara. Is Hollie there?"

"Uh, no, she's not," Matthew responded, stunned that the superstar was calling him. "I...uh...I haven't seen her." He hesitated, then asked, "Is there a reason you're looking for her? I know you two were involved—"

Mark broke in quickly. "Matthew, I assure you, I have no interest in Hollie. That's ancient history. I have a wife who means the world to me and I would never hurt her."

"She told me not to tell anyone where she was," the older man hesitated. "I don't know if—"

"She's involved with a drug dealer and an escaped felon," Mark snapped, feeling a fierce satisfaction when Matthew gasped. He had a sneaking feeling that the dot-com millionaire would be dumping her without a qualm, and good riddance. "If you know where she is..."

Matthew gave him the address, a seedy area of Los Angeles, without hesitation. Unknown to the singer, Felipe heard him repeat the address and realized what his brother was going to do.

"Marcos—" Felipe tried to stop him as Rosemary and Hannah looked on, but Mark was having none of it.

"No, Felipe, that bitch is going to hear from me!"

"At least let me come with you," Felipe begged him, putting out an arm.

Mark brushed him off impatiently. "This is between me and her." He was out the front door and in the Porsche before they could say a word.

"Where is he going, Felipe?" Mallory demanded. "I heard him mention Hollie."

Not liking the look in her cool green eyes, Felipe hesitated then said in a rush, "He found out she was the woman who helped Mendoza. He went to find her."

"What? *She* helped him? An innocent baby..." Thoughts were whirling through Mallory's mind so quickly she couldn't sort them out. Hollie, wondering where her accomplice was, Hollie, wanting revenge and money...

Hollie, out to hurt Mark.

That gold digger was not going to hurt her lamb. "What's the address, Felipe?"

"Tell her, sweetie," said Rosemary, moving to his other side.

Were they double teaming him? Feeling outnumbered, Felipe finally gave her the address, perplexed when Mallory told her twin sister, "Remember what we used to do in high school?"

"Oh, how could I forget." She snickered then said, "I'll change and meet you out front."

A dumbfounded Felipe watched as Rosemary, dressed identically to her twin, hurried downstairs. What on earth—"Rosemary," he began, putting out a hand to stop her.

"Trust me, sweetie, you don't want to know."

"Will you at least be careful?" he pleaded. "You're pregnant."

"Of course." She gave him a swift kiss and hurried out the door, unaware that her fiancée was planning to follow them.

Felipe stopped only to ask his parents to watch Carlie, then sped off in the BMW. They might have a head start but he knew exactly where to go. He and Marcos had stayed in that same area when they had first come to LA. He only prayed he would be in time.

In the courtyard of the ramshackle apartment building, Mark confronted his former girlfriend. He had caught her just as she was going out the door.

"You helped him kidnap my daughter?" Mark cried, disgusted at what she had turned into. "*Why?*"

"Hey, your brat means nothing to me. He said I could have the money."

"Well, you're going to have a hard time getting it. Mendoza is dead."

Hollie shrugged. "Pity."

I loved this? Mark shook his head in anguish. She had no morals either.

"You're as despicable as he was," he hissed, starting to turn around. He couldn't send her to prison; he would have to tell the police about the kidnapping and Mendoza's death. And how could he say Gabriel had inadvertently sent him into that ravine?

He couldn't do anything.

"Haven't you forgotten something, lover?"

Mark turned back to see she was holding a gun aimed at his chest.

"I want the money," Hollie sneered.

"How much farther?" Mallory said, not even stopping for the light.

"Turn left at the corner. It's that old complex on the right, the pink building."

"I see the Porsche." Mallory pulled into the cracked lot and ran from the car, Rosemary right behind her. They saw Mark leaning against a tree and moved forward, one on each side of the singer.

"What the hell?" the confused Hollie blurted.

"You bitch," hissed Mallory as Rosemary chimed in, "Money-hungry whore."

"Maybe your sugar daddy should know what you did."

"Taking up with a drug dealer," said Rosemary.

"Kidnapping innocent babies," added Mallory.

"We should tell him," Rosemary said.

"Yes, we should." Mallory nodded.

Hollie stared from one girl to another, feeling disoriented. Was there only one...or two?

She blinked and said dazedly, "There's only one of you, isn't there?"

"Is there?" Mallory asked.

"How many do you see?" Rosemary asked sweetly.

Their hair and clothes were identical, even their voices.

A speechless Mark listened in stunned silence as they continued their tormenting of Hollie, almost feeling sorry for her. He saw Felipe from the corner of his eye and motioned him into silence.

"What are they doing?" Felipe whispered.

"I don't know. I'm just glad they're not doing it to me."

They moved closer to Hollie.

"You called us Miss Fun Size," taunted Mallory.

"Don't you know good things come in small packages?"

They were so close—and so identical. Hollie had enough. She shrieked, dropped the gun, and took off running across the lot as fast as her stilettos would allow.

"We still got it, Mallie," said Rosemary jubilantly.

"Look at her go," Mallory snickered.

"Wonder twin powers activated?" Mark said, wiping the sweat from his forehead. He still leaned against the tree, holding it for support. He felt weak and drained, and reached out to take his wife's hand.

"Mark, I'm over here," said a still-giggling Mallory.

"She could have shot you," Mark protested, feeling sudden nausea wash over him. What on earth—

"Mark?" Mallory screamed, suddenly seeing the blood spread over his shoulder and running forward to help him.

He sagged to the ground as Felipe moved forward and caught him.

His brother all but threw him into the Porsche.

"What—"

"Lie back and keep still, Marcos. You're bleeding," Felipe cried, seeing the blood spreading over his brother's shoulder. He tossed the BMW keys at Rosemary. "You and Mallie meet us at the hospital."

"I'm what?" Mark twisted his head to look at his shoulder.

"The bitch shot you."

Agony

Was this a dream—a nightmare, actually?

Hands lifted him; someone cut the shirt from his bleeding shoulder. Mark felt the pinch of a needle, dimly heard the various voices discussing his condition.

Why did they sound so far away?

"Clean exit wound, but there's a lot of blood loss. We need more lap pads!"

There had been so much blood.

"Radial pulse weak and thready, heart rate up to 140, doctor!"

"More pressure, nurse."

He felt so very strange…colors fading in and out, and the lights were so bright—

"BP's dropping. He's going into shock—"

"Central line's in!"

The voices seemed even farther away.

"Pulse ox is dropping, he needs more oxygen."

Oxygen? But he was breathing, wasn't he?

Or was he already dead?

"We're losing him!"

Steve was leaning over him. "Mark, stay with us!"

"Squeeze in two units of O neg, stat!"

What had happened? Why was he lying here?

"We need to get him into the OR now! Let's move, people!"

And why was Gabriel looking over Steve's shoulder? Was he dead?

"No, Mark. We don't want you yet. You need to go back. Someone has to look after Adam, remember?"

"Hollie -shot me…"

"I know," said Gabriel gently. He pressed his hand to the open wound where the trauma doctor was trying to stop the bleeding.

'Scandal' was playing somewhere. He wanted to sing along but he couldn't.

"Mallory," Mark mumbled, wincing at the horrific pain.

Steve saw his friend's lips moving and seized his hand.

"Mark, don't you dare go toward that light!" Tears pooling in his eyes, he told the medical team, "He put me through med school…"

"Dr. Hanson," said a nurse, motioning at the wound in disbelief. The bleeding had slowed to a trickle.

"He can't die!"

"Gabriel," whispered Mark, staring at the archangel's gossamer wings.

They were so glittery. Had Adam's wings been like this?

"This is the last time you'll see me, Mark." He put a hand on the singer's cheek. "Go back."

"He's saying a name—Gabriel?"

Pain was holding his body hostage.

He didn't want to hurt anymore…so much pain-

"Go back!"

Suddenly, Mark heard himself groaning.

"BP is coming up, pulse coming down, and his color is improving." A disbelieving voice added, "You didn't even get the blood hung, Dr. Hanson. What happened?"

What, indeed. He couldn't explain any of this.

He opened his eyes to find Steve smiling at him tearfully.

"Amigo, I thought we lost you."

"This…is a hospital," said his confused friend, staring at him perplexedly.

"No, really? I realize that's a novel concept for you— you usually end up at my office, but Felipe at least has common sense, Mark."

~

In the waiting room, Felipe was fuming at Lieutenant Winslow. "I want that bitch arrested! She shot my brother in cold blood." He gave Winslow Hollie's name and address just as Mallory and Rosemary burst through the door.

"Where is he, Felipe?" Mallory cried, grabbing at him for support.

He quickly put an arm around his hysterical sister-in-law. "They're working on him, Mallie. He's got a whole medical team with him."

"Uh, which one…" began a confused Winslow, looking from one identical face to another.

"Rosemary, pull your hair back. I'm Mallory O'Hara," she told Winslow, taking a deep breath and trying to compose herself. "I remember you from the concert."

"Do any of you know what happened? Do you have any idea why she shot him?"

"She wanted his royalties from 'Scandal,'" Felipe answered.

Mallory looked at him in surprise. She felt his fingers tighten on her hand and knew he wasn't going to say anything about the kidnapping or Hollie's involvement.

"Why?"

"Because my husband wrote the song about her." She could play along. She didn't want to answer questions anyway. She wanted to see Mark.

"So she meets him, he refuses to give her money, she shoots him and runs off?" When Felipe nodded, Winslow asked, "And the gun?"

"Probably still in the parking lot." Rosemary said, giving him the address. "I saw her drop it."

"You were there?"

"We both were. Felipe too. But we didn't know then that Mark had been shot."

He watched them working on his arm, staring at the wound in fascinated horror.

"You and your needles," he murmured, wondering why the one in his hand didn't hurt. "Why am I getting sleepy?"

"Because I gave you a shot," Steve retorted.

"Could you bring Felipe here for a minute?"

"Not Mallie?"

"I need him first."

"He's probably talking to the police."

"We'll pick her up." Winslow eyed Felipe shrewdly. He was sure the younger man was holding something back but there was nothing to support it. "Strange we haven't been able to locate your old roadie, Mendoza. This is something I would have expected him to do. He had a gun."

"Which you have," Felipe said immediately.

"Yes, but…"

"Felipe," said Steve, his sudden appearance surprising them. "Mark wants to see you for a minute. Trauma room 1." As Mallory stared at him, the hurt in her green eyes, the physician swiftly assured her. "Honey, I think he just wants to ask him something. Then you can see him."

"Is he…" Mallory began, unsure what to ask. There had been so much blood.

"In a great deal of pain. They're stitching up his arm now. He's very lucky—the bullet just missed a major artery. I thought we were losing him." As Mallory gasped, Steve went on quietly, "He owes Felipe his life."

Tears were streaming down Felipe's ashen face as he gazed at Mark.

"Hey, I'm here, hermanito, thanks to you."

"Thanks to God!" Felipe blurted.

"He was here," Mark mumbled.

"God?" asked Felipe, confused.

"Gabriel. He told me to go back...said I had to look after Papa." Struggling against the drowsiness, he added, "You need to tell them."

"Of course I will."

"Don't...don't scare Mama. Don't let them know... know about Carlie..."

"Already taken care of. You rest now, Marcos." He started to go, but the faint pressure of his brother's fingers stopped him.

"Felipe..." Both eyes were closing but he wanted to tell him.

Felipe felt the tears fill his eyes again as Mark said faintly, "Tell McCoy I love him."

Swallowing the lump that was threatening his throat, he lightly pressed Mark's uninjured arm.

"He loves you too, Hatfield." He swiped the tears from his eyes and strode from the room blindly, nearly running into Steve.

"I want the truth, Steve. Is Marcos going to die?" he demanded.

"No, of course not. He could have, if it hadn't been for you. What brought this on?"

"He told me he loves me!"

"Felipe, Mark's never been in a hospital before. He's scared, he's nervous, and I imagine he does feel like he's cheated death again." Steve added quietly, "He told me about the knife wound. That must have been agony."

"Second time in my life that I've found my brother covered in blood." Felipe shuddered as the memory assailed him again. He added quietly, somberly, "But this time I have to tell our parents."

But it seemed someone already had. He was stunned to see Carlotta, rosary beads in hand, clutching Adam's arm as they hurried into the trauma center.

"Mama, how did you get here?"

"Ryan brought us. He is parking the car." Bottom lip trembling and tears coursing down her cheeks, she demanded of her younger son, "Felipe, please do not tell me fibs. Has Marcos died?" she blurted, her face drained of color.

"No, of course not," he assured her, repeating Steve's words. He put an arm around her hastily.

"He was shot in the arm and lost a lot of blood, but he'll be okay. Steve says he's scared and in a great deal of pain." Felipe managed a tiny smile. "But Marcos is a fighter. He'll pull through this."

Felipe wasn't quite sure how he knew this, but suddenly, words leaped into his ear, and he touched it gingerly. It reminded him of the day Adam had "spoken" to him in Loquesta.

And his father had noticed the gesture now.

"Gabriel spoke to you, laddie," he said when Carlotta was out of earshot.

"You mean whispered, don't you, Papa? Just like you used to." He added ruefully, "He's *spoken* to everyone else—I guess it was my turn." He managed a tiny smile as he pondered the archangel's words. "He said Marcos did it again—without any help from his parents this time." A startled expression crossed his face.

"And?" asked Adam. "There's something else; there always is with him."

"We told you your story is just beginning."

Acceptance

It was the day after the shooting.

"Are you going to let me out of here?" Mark demanded.

Steve looked up from the chart he was holding, a very satisfied smile on his face.

"Still trying, aren't you? I told you you're spending another night here, amigo."

"But I feel fine!" Well, except for this bullet wound.

"You were shot, Mark. You've got a hole in your shoulder." Crossing his arms, Steve eyed his friend sternly. "You aren't going anywhere." As Mark started to speak, his young doctor added sweetly, "Keep it up and I'll sic Carlotta on you."

"You would, wouldn't you?"

"And I would enjoy every minute of it, amigo."

As if on cue, Mark's petite mother appeared in the room. "You must listen to Dr. Steve, Marcos."

"He's a ghoul," muttered Mark.

"Should that not be Dr. Ghoul?"

"Thank you, Carlotta." Steve grinned.

"Do either of you realize that I have a concert tonight?"

"Felipe has taken care of it. He has also informed Mr. Greene and the news media. There are so many of them outside the hospital, Marcos," Carlotta said wonderingly. "What are paparazzis?"

"Vultures," said Steve, grimacing.

"They are? But they were so nice to Adam and me."

"Oh, my god." Mark's mouth sagged open in shock. With his free arm he reached out and grabbed Steve, yanking him closer. "Unless you want me to walk out of this hospital, get Felipe! Since he's now in charge of my life, he needs to run damage control."

"For what?"

"I can't tell you," Mark blurted, looking sideways at his innocent mother. "Will you please get him?"

"On my way."

As soon as he was out of earshot, he asked Carlotta, "Just what did you tell the nice reporters?"

"I told them I was your mother. They did not seem to believe me, Marcos," Carlotta said very indignantly. "I do not understand. One of them seemed to think I had an—eye lift?"

"They meant plastic surgery, Mama." His expression eased. "You didn't say anything about Carlie being kidnapped or Mendoza?"

"How can you lift your eyes?"

"Mama…"

"Marcos, I did not say anything inappropriate. I learned that as a messenger." Seeing the question poised on his lips, she added, "No, I did not mention that either. Of course, I do not know what Adam told them." She drew the sheet over him. "You must rest now. You are turning a very strange color."

"How can I rest, Mama? I've got holes in my arm, I'm full of drugs and needles, Steve won't let me leave, and you and Papa are giving interviews to the paps," Mark blurted, struggling with the uncomfortable hospital gown.

"She did nothing of the sort," Felipe said abruptly.

"Does Hank know you've replaced him, Felipe?" He turned his head away, but not before Felipe glimpsed the fear in his hazel eyes.

"Mama, why don't you find Dr. Steve and get some tea in the cafeteria?"

"You will take care of your brother?"

"Oh, I'll take care of him all right," Felipe said darkly.

Mark had covered his face with his hands. Felipe sat down in the chair beside the bed and reached over to touch his shoulder.

"What's got you spooked, Marcos? Possible damage to your arm, our parents loose in this hospital, or that you're depending on *me* for a change?" he asked shrewdly.

His hands dropped from his face.

"Try all of the above," Mark said finally. "And how come you know me so well?"

"Because I've known you the longest," Felipe retorted. "Let's see, you're worried you might not be able to play like before. I would think physical therapy could help."

"Maybe," Mark conceded. "I hadn't thought of that."

"No, of course not," Felipe snickered. "But I did. You're gonna have to realize that I have your best interests at heart. Lean on me—I'm perfectly capable, Marcos."

"I do realize it! I'm just not used—"

"To not being in control. I understand that. But it's just temporary." A hurt expression briefly slid across his face. "I can go back to little-brother mode anytime you're ready." There was a ghost of a smile on his face as he told Mark, "As for our parents, the last I saw of Papa he was examining a robot at the nurse's station, trying to figure out how it knew to get on the elevator. If he tries taking it apart…we may have a bill to rival the national debt. Mama was looking at the babies in the nursery."

"Oh," said Mark in a low voice.

Felipe focused cool blue eyes on him. "I realize my previous behavior might deem otherwise, but I know what I'm doing, Marcos. Give me *some* credit."

Hearing the coolness in his words, the superstar immediately protested, "Felipe, I've never—"

"Hello," said a small voice from the doorway.

Both brothers turned to see a little girl standing there—a child about ten years old and wearing a hospital gown. They watched as she plunked herself down in the other chair.

"I'm Maddie," she announced, regarding them in a friendly fashion.

Dear God, she was…she was *bald*, Mark saw, sudden tears filling his eyes.

"Hey, Maddie, I'm Mark and this is my brother, Felipe." He saw Felipe was also teary eyed. "It's nice to meet you. Are you a patient too?"

"Yep. I've been here a lot. I've got cancer but it's in remission," she said cheerfully. "You're new here." She gazed at him intently. "You're that singer the nurses keep talking about. Are you sick?"

"I was shot." Mark gestured to the bandage on his arm.

"Oh. Do you know One Way Ticket?"

"One Way Ticket?" Mark glanced at Felipe for an explanation.

"I think they're a new boy band, Marcos."

"No, Maddie, I don't know them, but if I did I'd have them come see you."

"Way cool."

"Your cancer is in remission, Maddie?" Felipe asked, his throat tight. How ironic. He had tried to kill himself, and this little girl was fighting for her life.

"Yep," she said again. "My daddy and I are celebrating. He said since my blood counts were good I could get this doll in the gift shop. She's beautiful," the little girl sighed.

"Where's your mama?" Mark asked softly.

"She died when I was born. It's just Daddy and me. I take care of him. He had to get a second job when I got sick," Maddie explained.

The singer turned to Felipe. "Could you get Steve?"

Felipe gave him a mystified look as he hurried out of the room, nearly bumping into the doctor.

"Mark, I am not releasing you."

"I'm not asking you to. Can I at least go for a walk with this young lady?"

"Where?" Steve asked suspiciously.

"Just to the gift shop. This is Maddie. We're getting her a doll. Maddie, this is Dr. Ghoul," he explained, leaning on Felipe as he helped him into a wheel chair.

"That's a funny name," said Maddie, staring at Steve.

"He's a funny patient. Are you going to keep an eye on him for me, Maddie? He might make a break for it."

"Doesn't he have a mommy either?"

"Oh, I have one. She's wandering around here somewhere looking for tea. Felipe?"

"I'll go find her. Then I'm going to find Maddie's father and offer him a job. We can always use another roadie." As Mark looked at him in surprise, Felipe said softly, "Best get used to it, Marcos. I've got a story to tell."

In a different part of Los Angeles, another story was coming to an end.

"You *canceled* my credit cards?" Hollie shrieked at Matthew.

"I also had the Mercedes picked up." He eyed her coldly, rebuking himself for being so stupid to get involved with this gold digger. "And the locks changed as well."

"Are you dumping me?" she cried, not caring if she made a scene or not.

"In a word, yes. Something I should have done long ago." His arms crossed, he snapped, "I'm running a business, Hollie. You, apparently are running around with drug dealers and ex felons. That won't do."

"Is this because of Mark?"

"It's because of you," retorted Matthew. Still surveying her coldly, he added, "According to the newswires he's been shot. They're looking for a blonde woman – with a butterfly tattoo on her cheek." His gaze slid to her right cheek. "You wouldn't know anything about that –would you?"

Trying not to show how much the question unnerved her, Hollie snapped, "And where would I get a gun?" She wished she could remember what she'd done with it. All she recalled was firing it at Mark. She could still see him clutching his chest, but what had happened to the gun? She couldn't remember anything after those twin tormentors accosted her.

"Don't you even care that he's been shot?" Matthew demanded.

"No. Why should I? He means nothing to me. And I don't care about you, either!"

"That's become very clear to me." His grey eyes gleamed with revenge. "I hope you realize that if you did shoot him and he doesn't survive, well, then you're in a great deal of trouble. A public figure like him," he shrugged. "You'll be in jail for a very long time. And I will say good riddance."

"I am not going to prison!"

"You can go to hell for all I care."

Two men telling her to go to hell in one day? I don't think so, Hollie vowed, searching Matthew's pockets for cash. As usual he had quite a bundle.

She yanked the cloth from the table and feverishly tried to wipe her fingerprints from the paperweight. She hadn't exactly meant to hit him, but when he said he was turning her in –

"I am not going to prison," Hollie echoed her earlier vow.

But if Mark some how survived and told everything to the cops, and if Matthew wasn't dead—

"I'll go to Mexico." She grabbed the key to Matthew's prized Mustang and shoved it in her pocket. She would leave the car at LAX and take the first flight to Cabo.

"They won't look for me there."

How do you know?

The soft words seemed to be echoing in her ear. Hollie looked around but she could see no one.

They're already looking for you, Hollie.

Thoroughly bewildered and frightened, she cried, "Who are you? How do you know my name?" Sweat ran down her face as she moved toward the door.

I know everything.

Her heart was pounding so hard she feared it would burst from her chest. She couldn't seem to catch her breath, either.

`   "I have to get out of here!" Spinning around, she was almost to the front door when the voice stopped her again. It seemed to be echoing off the walls.

Matthew isn't dead. You can get help for him.

"Why should I?" Hollie retorted, trying to turn the door knob. But it wouldn't turn.

So you would let him die, then.

"He was going to turn me in," she gasped as the pain exploded through her arm and chest. The breath faded from her body as she collapsed on the floor. She never saw Gabriel, his wings unfurled and his head bowed in sorrow as he gazed from Matthew to her.

"May God have mercy on your soul," the archangel said softly.

Epilogue

SALVATION

Steve was giving him a six-weeks checkup.

"I'm almost afraid to come in here. You might stick me with another needle," Mark said, looking at his young doctor dubiously.

"Behave or I will." Steve moved the singer's arm. "No stiffness or pain?"

"It feels fine. Once in a while there's a twinge but I think the therapy helped." He stared at his arm ruefully. "Look at me—a bullet hole in my arm."

"To match the one in your head. Whatever possessed you to go after that gold digger?"

"I was angry," he said simply. "There was no other reason."

Somberly, Steve added, "I suppose you saw her obituary? They said it was a massive heart attack."

"I read it," Mark said curtly.

"And that guy she was living with, Matthew. He's very lucky someone found him in time. Severe concussion –I suppose he slipped and hit his head," Steve mused.

Mark knew the truth about Matthew's injury. The dot com millionaire had paid him a surprise visit at Ambercrest and confirmed that Hollie had struck him —not caring if she killed him or not. He was going to turn her in, Matthew explained to Mark.

'I never knew what she was like. To just *–shoot* you –'

Justice had been served. 'She had no morals, Matthew,' he'd told him and the older man agreed. 'I'm just relieved you're not badly injured.'

'You, too,' Matthew had said, taking Mark's hand.

"You owe Felipe your life, Mark. If he hadn't gotten you to the hospital so quickly…" Steve shook his head, not wanting to remember what had almost happened.

"Breaking every rule of driving. I never knew he could drive so fast," Mark said, dimly recalling that wild ride to the hospital. As Steve released his arm, the singer added, "I take it I'm good to go?"

"You may. You're in perfect health." He eyed the tiny smile hovering around his friend's mouth. "You're up to something, amigo."

"Yes, I am, and I need your help. I need a drummer."

The curious physician answered, "I still play. But I don't understand why you would need me. You've got Ryan."

"Ryan's going to be playing keyboard."

"But Felipe…" Steve's puzzled words trailed off.

"I think Jonathan told me he can play harmonica. Oh, Felipe?" Mark's grin grew bigger. "That's my surprise, amigo."

A week later, Steve, Jonathan, and other past and present members of Rhythm Nation were backstage at The
Reese Martin Show, waiting for Mark to arrive. Aside
from Felipe, they all seemed to know what was going
on, a fact that hadn't escaped the keyboardist.

"What are you guys up to?" Felipe asked, bewildered
by the little smiles he had seen. "This isn't like Marcos.
He booked himself on this show—when he's never
done a talk show in his life."

"Mark swore us to secrecy." Evan tried to smother
his own smile.

"Good, we're all here." Mark, followed by Adam,
Carlotta, Mallory, and Rosemary, appeared backstage;
his customary formal clothes replaced by casual denim.
He handed Carlie over to Mallory as he spotted the
excited Maddie by her father.

"How's my favorite roadette?" He knelt down and
hugged her.

"Mark, I'm getting my hair back!"

"You sure are, Maddie. Dr. Ghoul says you're doing
great." He gestured at Steve.

"Thanks to you," said the little girl's grateful father.

The embarrassed singer said quickly, "She's doing all
the work. You've got an awesome little girl there." He
laid a hand on the young roadie's shoulder. "We have to
take care of her."

Seeing Evan approaching, Mark added, "Everything
good to go, Evan?"

"All set, amigo. And Felipe doesn't know a thing." He eyed him carefully. "You feel okay?"

"I feel fantastic." The band fell into place as Reese Martin said with a hush in his voice, "I still can't believe whom I'm about to introduce. He's never done a talk show and I'm very honored to have him and Rhythm Nation with us tonight. Ladies and gentlemen, Mark O'Hara!"

The curtain parted, and Mark said a swift prayer as he took the microphone his new roadie handed him.

A very puzzled Felipe watched as his now fully recovered brother effortlessly and eloquently went through the verses of "Love is When I Loved You." So far everything seemed normal—it was no different than any other concert. How then to explain the secretive glances between Marcos and Evan, or the little grin his brother wore? He was even introducing the band, Felipe discovered, wondering why Evan was suddenly beckoning to him.

More and more curious. Were they *all* in cahoots with Marcos? Ryan got up from his drums only to have Steve take his place. Oddly enough, Jonathan was now holding a harmonica.

What the devil was going on?

And why was Marcos talking to the audience?

Mic in hand, Mark moved to the edge of the stage.

"A short time ago I was shot." As the audience let out a collective gasp, Mark added wryly, "I guess I forgot to duck. It's only by the grace of God and an awesome medical team, including my doctor, Steve Hansom, that I'm alive. Them—and my brother; I owe my life to him." He looked back at Evan and nodded. "Felipe, this is for you."

On cue, the band broke into "He Ain't Heavy, He's My Brother."

A bewildered and overcome Felipe focused his tearful blue eyes on Marcos and wondered what to do. He eyed Adam helplessly and his father gestured at Mark.

Reese Martin had tears sliding down his face, Mallory and Rosemary were both crying; even the band members were teary eyed as Mark's hauntingly beautiful voice flowed over them.

Felipe joined in the words as he moved forward and put his free arm around him.   They were in this journey together.

In the gold-starred dressing room, Carlotta had her rosary in hand, her lips moving in a silent prayer as she glanced periodically at her granddaughter in her portable playpen. That there was another being in the room, a magnificent angel with white, gossamer wings, was only apparent to the cooing baby. Gabriel smiled down at her.

"I couldn't let him die, could I, Carlie?"

"Ga!" shrieked Carlie, clapping her hands.